DANGER BOY

DANGER BOY

Ancient Fire

Mark London Williams

CANDLEWICK PRESS
CAMBRIDGE, MASSACHUSETTS

Copyright © 2001, 2004 by Mark London Williams

Danger Boy® is a registered trademark of Mark London Williams.

First Candlewick Press paperback edition 2006

The Library of Congress has cataloged the hardcover edition as follows:

Williams, Mark London.
Danger boy: ancient fire / by Mark London Williams. — 1st ed.
p. cm.
Summary: When twelve-year-old Eli becomes involved with the time travel experiments that the government pressures his parents to pursue, he travels to fifth-century Alexandria, Egypt, where he meets Thea, a scholar accused of sorcery, and Clyne, an extraterrestrial saurian who is working on a homework assignment.
ISBN 0-7636-2152-8 (hardcover)
[1. Time travel — Fiction. 2. Alexandria (Egypt) — Antiquities — Fiction. 3. Egypt — History — Greco-Roman period, 332 B.C.–640 A.D. — Fiction. 4. Dinosaurs — Fiction. 5. Fathers and sons — Fiction.] I. Title.
PZ7.W66697Dan 2004
[Fic] — dc21   2003043774

ISBN 0-7636-3092-6 (paperback)

10 9 8 7 6 5 4 3 2

Printed in the United States of America

This book was typeset in Cygnet Roman.

Candlewick Press
2067 Massachusetts Avenue
Cambridge, Massachusetts 02140

visit us at www.candlewick.com

Dedicated, with love and thanks,
to Elijah, muse and inspiration,
and Asher, his companion in adventure
M. L. W.

Prologue

The year is 415 of our "Common Era." Still early in the first millennium. It's night and there's fire on the water.

The flames come from a burning fleet of ships, which are sinking in the harbor. Some of the pitch—the tar that seals up the boats and makes them leakproof—is melting off in little globs and drifting over the waves. The globs still burn as they float away, lighting up the water like rows of lanterns at a party.

But this isn't the kind of party you'd want to get invited to: The fire has spread to shore, moving from the boats to the docks to the Royal Quarter beyond, shooting through the city like a deadly, fast-moving vine. The flames are even heading out to the dikes and levees that separate the necropolis—the city of the dead, the burial grounds—from the rest of the city. Where the dead are getting no rest at all.

The splintering wood from the dikes has allowed the seawater to rush in and sweep the mummified bodies out on the waves, setting them adrift like rotting boats moving toward the lighthouse. Toward a very scared thirteen-year-old girl, who finds herself surrounded not only by the fire but also by an angry mob of people who want to hurt her.

Onshore, the fire races toward the Royal Quarter, toward the place inside it that had been her home: a large complex the locals call both a library and a museum. As far as anyone knows, this library has the single largest collection of books on Earth. In the year 415, it's very hard to make a book: Each of them is really a scroll, hand-printed on papyrus or dried animal skin.

It's difficult to make books, yet this library has nearly half a million of them: nearly all the ideas anybody has about art, math, science, philosophy; copies of famous plays and poems.

All in one place. All at one time.

The fire closes in.

And if the library burns—when it burns—all the ideas, the plays, the poems, will burn with it. Most of them will disappear forever, vanishing with even less of a trace than the mummies bobbing in the water by the docks.

Someone else has escaped the fire, too, and is trying to make his way to the lighthouse. He travels through the burning city, only to be taken prisoner again: a boy, about twelve years old. Like the girl, he's both scared and brave.

Somewhere else in the fire and flood is another person. Except this person is a human-sized lizard, quite comfortable walking on two feet and talking. His name is Clyne. Versed in human tongues, he's been mistaken for a demon. And he's part of *the reason the girl in the lighthouse is in so much trouble now, accused of being a sorceress.*

She doesn't know what Clyne really is, but he's not a demon. One word the boy used to describe him was "dinosaur."

Out in the lighthouse tower, the girl waits desperately for the boy. Or the lizard. Someone who's on her side. It's her city that's burning: Alexandria, Egypt, on the shores of the Mediterranean Sea.

The girl's name is Thea, which means "moon." Like the moon, she's trying to conjure light at night and make the lighthouse come alive, casting its great beams off the mirrors inside the tower, which aim back out toward the city. With light, someone will know she's there. But the city is covered by its own light as the flames grow stronger.

In the year 415, this lighthouse on the tiny island called Pharos is the tallest building on Earth. But it may not be tall enough: The people who've surrounded it are using a battering ram on the doors below, and eventually they'll break in. The crowd's leader scares Thea more than the

fire, more than the bodies floating in the water:
He's a monk named Tiberius. Yesterday—the last
day of Thea's old, regular life—he came for her
mother, Hypatia, and dragged her through the
streets.

Hypatia used to be the head librarian. According to Tiberius, she knew too much about too
many things. Especially for a woman.

Thea just barely escaped the same fate herself.
She's pretty sure she won't be able to escape the
mob a second time.

Right now, Thea's main hope is that the boy
with the strange speech and strange clothes can
somehow figure out a way to get to her and
maybe help her vanish into thin air for a while—
the same way he does.

The mob howls below: "Thea!" "Witch!"

Thea looks out across the water as burning
pieces of ship drift toward the island and toward
the city, occasionally colliding with the dead. She
thinks that if she looks hard enough, she just might
see something, some tiny speck of something that

she recognizes. Something familiar despite all the fire and terror in the air.

She closes her eyes a minute and summons up faces to give her strength: her mother's face, the lizard man's, and the boy's. The boy is even wearing his funny hat. He told her what it was, but the words made no sense: a "baseball cap."

But how could they make sense? That kind of hat won't be invented for almost another fifteen hundred years.

And the boy himself hasn't even been born yet.

Chapter One

Eli: Secrets for Trees

August 1, 2019 C.E.

"He's not a weapon! He's my *son*!"

"No, Sands, you're wrong! In somebody else's hands, he *is* a weapon! He's dangerous!"

"Is that why you gave me that stupid 'Danger Boy' name?"

We're having a three-way argument, and there's a long pause after I say that.

My name isn't Danger Boy, but Eli Sands, and I'm a time traveler. That's the easiest way to think of it—though, of course, being yanked around through history is never easy. I like to think of it more as being "tangled up in time," 'cause each time you make the journey, your life gets more and more complicated.

The two men yelling are my dad, Sandusky Sands (I don't know about that name, either. My grandparents must've had a weird sense of humor.), and Mr. Howe.

Mr. Howe works for the government, in a department called Black Box because it has no real name. It's a secret division of something that *does* have a name: DARPA—the Defense Advanced Research Projects Agency.

My dad's a physicist—or at least he was— and Mr. Howe had been watching his experiments for a long time. After Mom's accident, Mr. Howe practically took over our lives.

Right now, he's staring at me. Then he stares at my dad.

"You told him the code name?"

"I showed him the whole file."

"You showed him the *Danger Boy* file?"

"I don't have any secrets from my son."

"Every parent should keep some secrets from his children."

"Not every parent does to his family what I've done to mine." My dad's thinking about my mom again. About the fact she's disappeared.

I look at both men and think, *Will you shut up?* but I don't say it. My dad and Mr. Howe have been going at it like this for a while now. Years, really. If I walk right out of the room, I bet neither of them will notice.

"Eli! Get back here!" That's Mr. Howe. I guess they *did* notice.

But I ignore them and keep on going down the hall. Well, it's not really a hall; it's a limestone cave, inside an abandoned winery, which is where I live now. The winery is in the Valley of the Moon, near a town called Sonoma, in California. They make a lot of wine around here, which probably won't surprise you, but our particular winery has been turned into a lab, which might.

At least my room is normal.

It has all the things you'd expect to see in a kid's room: Gaming Guild stuff—like roam boxes — a lot of stray vidpads, baseball cards, old clothes, a box of cookies, and my gene map tacked up on the wall. Another wall is just for Comnet. Their version of Comnet. They've set it up so they can track any personal messages that come or go.

It's been that way since I got back. And I've only been back about a week.

There's also stuff in my room that's not normal, like that little statue of the bull man with the snakes around his legs, over there on my desk. I suppose he could be an action figure, like maybe from one of the Guild games. But he's not. He's made of clay, and he's supposed to be a god of some sort, called Serapis, and he was big stuff back in Alexandria.

That's where I got him. In Alexandria, Egypt.

Well, not that exact statue. The DARPA guys took the original as evidence. Proof of my travels. Two days later Mr. Howe gave me this duplicate. "A little gesture of good faith" was the way he put it.

You can still find Alexandria on a map, too, but that's not the original, either. The city I know is mostly underwater now.

But not when I was there, more than sixteen hundred years ago. Which, like I say, for me has been about a week.

It's been a *long* week.

But that's what happens when you're a time traveler.

I can try to tell you about it, but when you become unglued in time, tangled up in it, you lose track of where the "beginning" is.

And the idea of where it might end still scares me. I think they want to send me back there. To Alexandria.

At least, Mr. Howe does. I hear him talk to my dad: People are getting sick; strange things are happening to time itself, and people like Mr. Howe are getting worried. They think I can help make it all better.

I'm just a twelve-year-old kid who likes baseball and vidpad games. Why me?

Well, I know why. It's because of my dad's time spheres, and the fact that my mother disappeared into one, and the additional fact that *I* disappeared into one, too, except I came back.

They've tried to keep me around the lab since I returned — Mr. Howe and his DARPA team watching me the whole time, checking up and monitoring me. Actually, I'm amazed they've let me be in my room alone this long without asking —

"Eli? How are you feeling?"

It's Mr. Howe again, with some guy in a doctor coat who I don't recognize. There've been a lot of guys I don't recognize hanging around lately.

"I'd feel better if I could get out of here. Take a walk. See a baseball game. Get some food. Anything. Even go to school."

"We can't let you go back to school now. You're in a special circumstance."

"I'd feel better if you and Dad would quit fighting."

"Your dad, Eli, doesn't realize how much good you can do."

"Why are you calling me Danger Boy? That's a corny name."

"When you do important work like ours, Eli—like yours—it's good to have a code name. Just in case."

"Is 'Mr. Howe' a code name, too?"

He doesn't answer, and instead picks up the Serapis statue. "This souvenir you brought back—we should really give it to a museum. Someday."

"You mean the original? That one's a fake."

Mr. Howe puts it back on my desk, gingerly. "Right."

Serapis was supposed to be a god of healing, but I didn't see too much healing back in Alexandria. The city felt like it was about to explode.

Now the doctor guy is shining a light in my eye. "Hey!"

Mr. Howe waves him away. "Later."

"Where's my dad?"

"He actually *is* out for a walk. Said he needed to think things over."

"How come *he* gets to go?" I ask for the zillionth time that week.

"Because he's not under medical observation. Because he didn't just become the first person who we know can time-travel."

Now Mr. Howe sits down on the bed only a couple feet away and turns to look at me. He's supposed to be all sincere, but his expression gives me the creeps.

"Eli, you do know how special you are, right? Nobody wants to hurt you, but you have a chance to help a lot of people. To be a part of history yourself."

"Starting with slow pox, huh?"

"Starting with slow pox, and helping us find a cure. We need to know if you'd be willing to go back again. This time, on purpose."

"I want to find my dad first." I get up and head for the door and hear the doctor guy behind me. "Sir. He's not supposed to go outside yet. Not by himself."

"He'll be all right," Howe says. Which means they're going to have me followed. "Eli, please stay close by."

As soon as I get outside, I see another DARPA guy, this one in a blue uniform. He looks at me kind of unhappily, but I keep walking toward the thicket of oaks nearby and hope I can disappear before he starts to follow.

When I make it into the stand of trees, I begin to run down the path. I don't know if my dad came this way or not. I'm trying to get to a place called Wolf House, a couple miles from here.

Way back last century, some guy who wrote adventure books owned it—a big old stone house in the middle of the woods that looked like it was raised up out of the earth.

At least, that's how it was supposed to look, but it all burned down the night before the adventure-book guy and his wife were supposed to move in. It's a big ruin now, and they made a kind of park around it, so you could have a nice picnic where someone else's dreams were all broken up.

I like to sneak into the park without paying and go there to think.

Maybe my dad's going there, too. If I can find him, it'll be the first time we've been alone together . . . since Mr. Howe showed up. Maybe we can talk.

But I don't want any of these DARPA guys hanging around. I'm running pretty hard now, but so's the guy in the blue uniform, and when I look back, he's yelling something into his headset, so I guess my days—or minutes—of outside walks are gonna be numbered.

This could be my only chance to get away for a while. But if I stay on the path, it's gonna be too obvious to the DARPA guys where I'm headed.

"Dad! Dad!"

No answer. He could be anywhere.

The blue uniform is catching up. I come

around a bend, then cut in fast through the brush, down toward the creek. If I can get deep enough in the bushes, he won't be able to see me. . . .

Aw, nuts. But they have equipment that can amplify my heartbeat. They can hear me, even if they can't see me.

This sucks. Can't I just be by myself for a little bit?

As I move through the trees, some low branches scratch my face. One of them drags behind my ear, over my neck.

There's a strange tingling, almost like a sudden, intense sunburn. I reach back to feel my skin, and my fingertips tingle, too, when they touch a small rough spot the size of a quarter.

I look at my fingertips. I can feel the substance. Because it blends in so well with my skin — it looks like a slight bruise — the doctors have missed it. And since everyone here speaks English, I forgot I had it on.

My lingo-spot.

A lingo-spot is a plasmechanical device for

translating languages. *Plasmechanical* means something that's half biology and half technology.

How do I know all that?

A dinosaur told me.

But I don't want to explain any of this to Mr. Howe or DARPA, so I start wiping off my lingo-spot on the bark of another tree. It looks like it's a redwood.

Then I wonder if the lingo-spot will suddenly help the tree understand human beings. Let it hear our secrets.

But that would mean, what? Translating words into sap? Into the rustle of leaves? How do you make a language out of that?

I jump at what sounds like a burp, but there's no one around. It seemed to come from the direction of . . .

. . . the tree. Like the lingo-spot made a noise.

At least, that's what I hope it was.

I move a little farther away. Even if the redwood could hear secrets, it wouldn't matter.

Not with mine: They're doozies. Like the dinosaur I just talked about.

I originally met him in a place called the Fifth Dimension.

Ah, forget it. The tree wouldn't believe me, either.

Chapter Two

Eli: Snowball Fight
June 7, 2019 C.E.

Even before I got tangled up in time, I'd been to a lot of places.

Like, for example, the Motel Bayou Deluxe, outside New Orleans. My dad and I had a snowball fight there, and I hit two grand slams in one inning.

"You know, it never really used to snow in New Orleans, especially in summer. But the weather seemed to make a lot more sense when I was a kid."

My dad was using that phrase a lot back then, "when I was a kid." It's a way grownups have of talking when the present moment has them kind of mixed-up or sad.

Dad was actually pretty happy during the snowball fight, even when I ambushed him by hiding under our parked truck with an armful of icy ammo and pelting him on his back and head when he walked by. He actually laughed. He hadn't done that in ages.

"You're getting sneaky, Eli. I don't know if that's a good thing."

"It's good for stealing bases. Or if I ever decide to become a spy."

Sometimes, you have to be careful what you joke about.

Dad and I were driving cross-country, moving out of my hometown of Princeton, New Jersey. He'd inherited the old winery out in the Valley of the Moon from some uncle or something, and it sat there for a couple years, empty and abandoned, till my dad decided he'd had enough of Jersey and was going to try things out in California.

I'd never lived anywhere else but Princeton.

It's where I grew up and where my best friend, Anderson Wall, lived. Andy. "Wall, wall, cracks on the wall." I think that was the first thing I'd ever said to Andy. We were in second grade and had just met on the playground. When you're little like that, the idea of moving away never really crosses your mind.

I was born in Princeton because that's where the Institute for Advanced Study was. The Institute was run by Princeton University and was supposed to be a place where scientists and thinkers could sort of noodle around and goof off and come up with stuff on their own, without any outside pressure. Einstein worked there back in the twentieth century.

My dad and mom worked there in the twenty-first.

Dad was good with spacetime. I don't mean *space* and *time* but *spacetime*. One word for two sides of the same cosmic thing—ways to try and figure out where you are on the humongous map of the universe, like north and south. Except spacetime is *where* and *when*.

Since his grad school days, he'd been tinkering with spacetime, changing the electrical charges of particles—the tiniest pieces of the universe, the bits that make up atoms. Dad figured out how to accelerate them through space and send them backward—not just through the air, but backward in time, too.

That's how he met my mom, Margarite, who was pretty good with spacetime herself.

With her help, Sandusky had perfected his first "spacetime sphere"—a small area, the size of a basketball, maybe, surrounded by, well, kind of a force field. That's what it'd be called in one of those corny old sci-fi movies, anyway. Especially since it was pumped out by a constantly humming generator.

Inside the force field, time moved differently. You could put a banana in there, and it wouldn't get soft and mushy for days. Sometimes weeks. Because time was moving slower for the banana.

Dad thought the little spheres could have practical uses—like keeping an organ fresh if you were waiting to transplant it, or storing blood for a transfusion. You could slow down disease cells and study them.

All kinds of uses like that.

Word about his experiments got out, and one day Mr. Howe showed up. I was pretty young, maybe around seven. He would come by the lab, and he would also come by the house. He tried to act the way some long-lost uncle would—way too friendly and smiling too much.

I guess things started to change for my parents at the Institute, too. They couldn't do their experiments just for the sake of finding stuff out. Mr. Howe wanted everything to have a purpose.

He was full of ideas: Like, he wanted to start putting live animals inside the spheres and running tests on them, to see if their aging could be slowed down.

Dad said he wasn't ready to put living creatures inside his time sphere. I remember one particular argument he had with Mr. Howe.

Both of them were standing in the backyard after dinner on a really cold October evening, and I could hear them through the closed window in my room.

It was the first time they had their "weapon" argument.

Sandusky said he wasn't going to use his science to hurt people or make war. Mr. Howe just kind of laughed at that. He said something about how the time sphere wasn't really a weapon at all, it'd just be helping his country.

A lot of things started to go wrong in a hurry after that.

Mom stopped going into the lab with Dad so much, which meant I got to see more of her in the afternoons when I came home from school.

Those were pretty good times — when I felt like a regular kid, just getting along in my life.

Andy and I had joined a Gaming Guild to be part of our favorite Comnet game, Barnstormers. It's a baseball game with monsters. See, you pick a squad of "Barnstormers," creatures who go around the country on a team bus, playing pickup ballgames in small towns or challenging minor-league teams to matches. Like a scarier version of a fantasy baseball league.

The kind of monsters you pick affects how you play: Like, if you have a lot of vampires, you can only play at night. If you have too many zombies, they run slow and you don't have base speed. Werewolves? They can really keep their eye on the ball—but watch out for full moons. And if you beat the local team, you'll probably be chased out of town. With torches.

You can trade players, and even play league games on the Net. Andy and I just did it for fun.

There was a place on the edge of town called Herronton Woods. Andy and I rode our bikes together all the way down Nassau Street and spent afternoons there. There was a spot we liked in the middle of all the oaks—some kind of plant disease had swept through there a few years back. In one area, where they had chopped down the sick trees, it made a kind of creepy clearing, full of stumps and twisted branches.

We liked to go and stay till late afternoon, when the shadows would get long, because the area reminded us of a place where some Barnstormers might really play a game—a little spooky, but still with enough room to hit a ball around.

Andy and I would play some real ball— usually a version of over-the-line, with oak stumps to mark the different kinds of hits you could get—and then we'd take out our roam boxes.

Roam boxes let you capture extra-rare characters that weren't available on your vidpads. The characters were signals you could only pick up in a certain area, sort of like the way my dad describes old TV broadcasts or something. In other words, you could only receive them in a specific place. There were thousands of Barnstormer characters all over the country. You could pick them up in shopping malls, parks, schoolyards—anywhere anyone wanted to make one up or sponsor one. But you had to have a roam box, and you had to be standing in the right spot.

In Herronton Woods, someone kept making up Barnstormer characters, like the Jersey Devil—who was actually a good shortstop—and the Pine Barrens Thing—who was slow, but a fair catcher. Then they would put them out in the air for someone to catch in a roam box.

Andy and I never figured out who was behind it—there was no ad that went with any of the new characters—and there wasn't always a new player to catch every time we went out there, but part of the fun was never knowing what might be lurking in the woods. It felt cool, like you were actually inside the game a little bit.

So Andy and I were out there, with our roam boxes and gloves and bats and balls, pretending to be Barnstormers ourselves, about four o'clock on a November afternoon, and this is one of the last great memories I have of my mom, before everything just got really bad and confused.

I remember it the way grownups say they remember things: suddenly, with no warning, triggered by some movement in the light, or a smell or something, anything that takes you back to that crystal-clear place in your memory, which isn't really what's happening to you right then, but comes from some earlier time. Which is sort of like being in a time machine, too.

When my mom showed up, she was all bundled up in a coat and actually looked kind of pretty right then, in a way that wasn't too corny. Kind of like herself and not just a mom.

"What are you doing here?"

She smiled at us. "There's a storm coming in pretty fast. I didn't think you'd have time to make it back to the house, so I brought the truck. You can throw your bikes in back."

When we slid into the front seat, I saw

some cookies there on a paper plate. Molasses cookies, which she'd just made. They were still warm.

"Mom . . ." I wasn't sure if I should be embarrassed in front of Andy, if the cookie thing *was* too corny.

"'Thanks, Mom,'" she said, trying to imitate me.

"Hey, thanks, Margarite!" Andy never passed up a chance to have a snack.

"You're welcome, Andy," she said in her regular voice, giving me a little elbow in the side.

It had clouded up by then, and right after that the ice storm began. We watched the slush fall against the windshield.

After we dropped Andy off, my mom got out, grabbed a fistful of ice from off the truck, plopped back down on her seat, and shut the door behind her.

"First snowball of the season," she said.

"It's not really snow, Mom."

"That's okay. We don't really have seasons anymore, either. Let's take this home and put it in the freezer, and we'll use it when we get some real snow." She set it up on the dashboard.

We never did have that snowball fight. Some things you shouldn't put off. The next thing my mom said was, "Your dad wants me to start helping at the lab again."

It had something to do with Mr. Howe. He'd gotten his hands on a rare particle that isn't normally found on Earth—it was discovered inside the air pocket of some kind of space rock—and given it to Dad.

Dad had been wanting to create a bigger kind of time sphere by re-creating the conditions in the early universe, like a really tiny big bang—which is how the whole idea of time got started anyway.

Think about it—who kept track of time before everything was created? If nothing was there, why would you need to? No endings to anything, no "after"—just one great big long "before"—until the universe cooled off and there were galaxies and places and stories to go with them.

So with the chance to use rare particles in his experiments, Dad actually let himself get talked into something by Mr. Howe. I guess Dad figured he could keep control of the situation, but it didn't work out that way.

Sandusky also needed Margarite's help. She was better at splitting atoms than he was.

She finally agreed to do it, so they were both getting talked into something they weren't sure they should do. They say kids pressure each other that way a lot, but I don't think it's just kids.

It was later, when my mom was working by herself in the lab, that the explosion happened. They never found her. No body, nothing. She just disappeared.

My dad stopped all work on the time sphere. Over the next few weeks, he barely talked to anybody, including me.

The weeks turned into months, then a year. And there was still no trace of my mom. But for a long time, my dad kept acting like she could return at any moment. Our lives were kind of frozen with the terrible, sudden loss of her.

It was a piece of paper—a tax bill on an abandoned winery my dad had inherited in California—that finally helped him decide he'd had just about enough of New Jersey. The winery was called Moonglow, because of the Valley of the Moon.

I guess I was ready for some kind of change, too. I hardly ever went to Herronton Woods anymore, and Andy didn't seem to come by all that much.

When my dad and I drove out of Princeton in our truck, there were fierce storms in the Midwest, so we weren't able to take a direct route to California. We headed south, and that's how we wound up in New Orleans.

There'd been snow on the ground for a few days by the time we got there, and I'm not sure what it was that finally broke through my dad's mood during *that* snowball fight. But I was glad to see him back, at least a little bit. The way I remembered him. Kind of the time-machine effect again.

In the motel room, I unrolled my vidpad. Maybe Andy had sent me an e-package; we promised to try and keep in touch when we were saying goodbye, but again, all the weather was making it difficult for some of the messages to go through.

So I wound up playing a short Barnstormer game with some local kid with the screen name SpudRuckus, and that's how I hit two grand slams in one inning.

SpudRuckus had a lot of zombies and what he called swamp critters on his team, and no real pitching, so it wasn't all that hard to load up the bases and hit one out. Still, I felt kind of proud.

When I went to tell my dad about it, he'd already fallen asleep on the big double bed. But there was a smile on his face. And then I remembered how my mom smiled that day in the woods, with the ice storm coming.

And I wondered if my dad was dreaming. Maybe in his dreams, he found a way to be with my mom again.

Chapter Three

Eli: Driving through Thunder
June 9, 2019 C.E.

We left New Orleans the next day. One of the museums was having a pirate exhibit that I really wanted to see, but Dad wasn't stopping for anything.

We ate breakfast in the truck, driving along, with just the quiet buzz of the electric motor joining our chewing and sipping noises as we ate beignets and drank chicory coffee.

Beignets are those special donuts they make in New Orleans that are covered with powdered sugar and don't have holes in the middle.

"Your mom and I came down here before you were born," Dad said after a few minutes. "When we were both still in grad school. The first morning here, we had beignets and coffee, just like this."

I don't know why grownups like coffee—it's really bitter—but after I put enough milk and sugar in it, it tasted okay. Actually, this was the first time I'd ever had it—to my surprise, Dad just nodded when I asked if I could order some, too. And hearing him then, I wondered if it was his memory of that time with my mom that made it important to know there was still someone around he could order a second cup of coffee with, even if it was just a twelve-year-old kid.

"Dad? What really happened with Mom in the lab? You and Mr. Howe told me she disappeared, but people don't disappear in explosions—they get hurt. Or they die."

He stopped chewing his beignet. I could tell Dad was getting uncomfortable.

"This was a different kind of explosion, Eli.

31

It was an explosion of *time.*" Now it was my turn to stop chewing.

"It has to do with your work?"

"It's not my work anymore. That's why we're going to California."

We were both quiet again, and Dad just kept heading west. Eventually, he turned on the satellite scanner to listen to a music station out of West Africa that he really likes. I unrolled a vidpad to check messages—just ads, nothing from Andy—and see if I could pick up another Barnstormer game.

The weather kept doing weird things, so the Comnet links weren't very reliable, and eventually I just read some stuff I'd stored in one of my files, on twentieth-century minor-league baseball teams.

The weather was pretty wild during the whole drive; our storm siren kept going off, which meant we had about fifteen minutes to pull over or adjust course before the next cloudburst hit. Bad weather had been hovering over the Midwest and was shifting south toward us, so we had to zig while it zagged. Instead of heading straight through Texas, and then New Mexico and Arizona, we wound up on a road my dad called old Route 66 and spent an afternoon and part of a night in a place called Vinita, Oklahoma.

The clouds were dark, and there were streaks of lightning coming out of the sky when we pulled into town.

We saw a flickering electric sign that said CABIN CREEK MOTEL. We both ran from the truck into the main office, and since there weren't any other cars around, figured that getting a room would be pretty easy.

When we stepped in, we heard a strange tapping sound, not quite like hammering— more like somebody knocking two small rocks together with a steady rhythm. "Shhh. Listen to that," my dad said, holding up a hand. "Typing."

"Typewriter typing?" I don't think I'd ever

seen a typewriter before, except in pictures. I know people used to write on them, while they were waiting for computers to be invented. Of course, hardly anybody writes on a computer anymore, either. They usually just speak into their vidpads and print it out somewhere later, if they still need it down on paper.

My dad just stood there listening a minute before ringing the bell.

Eventually the tapping stopped, and a man came out of the back. Older than Dad, with sandy gray hair and a square jaw, he stared at us through a pair of old-fashioned wire-rim glasses that magnified his eyeballs so that the most casual expression on his face seemed really intense. He looked at us like we had stepped out of a dream and he was having a hard time believing we were there.

"It's *you*," he said at last, looking right at me. Neither my dad nor I knew what to say.

"Well, yes, it's us," Dad finally answered. "And we'd like a room."

The man nodded, and with the tiniest hint of a smile, slid a large guest book across the counter. "You coming here, or passing through?"

"Passing through." My dad shrugged.

"We all pass through don't we?" the man said with that sudden, intense eyeball-look as he stared at my father.

The man gave Dad an old-fashioned ink pen, and it was Sandusky's turn to stare — at the antique in his hand. Then he signed us in.

"Room number one," the man said. "Right next door."

My dad took the key without speaking, and we ran out into the rain and then let ourselves into the room.

Stepping inside and flipping on the light, we could see the place was fixed up to have a Civil War theme from two centuries back, but that wasn't the unusual thing. At the foot of the bed was a *TV*!

I don't mean a wall monitor, but an old, bulky television in its own wood cabinet, standing on four legs, and plugged into the wall—like straight out of a museum. It even had preprinted numbers on the dial . . . and it only went up to channel thirteen!

Not expecting anything to happen, I flipped the *on* switch, and after nearly a minute of flickering light, a big eye-looking symbol came on, and then there was a serious-looking man reading the news. He was showing films of soldiers somewhere in a jungle.

My dad looked at it, then turned the dial to a different channel. There wasn't much on, and it was all black-and-white. I guessed there was some local festival of old shows on. Dad stepped away and watched the screen, then stepped up close again and grabbed the round wire loop from the top of the set. Suddenly, the picture got fuzzy, like when your local satellite link goes bad.

"That's it," he said under his breath. "Wait here."

He left the room, but I went after him.

Who wants to be left alone in a strange place dressed up to look like a nearly two-hundred-year-old war?

When I stepped into the office, Dad was hitting the bell over and over. The typing had stopped again, and the man with the big eyes came out from the back.

"I hear you," he said.

"That television," my dad said, sounding both excited and mad, "seemed to be receiving broadcast signals through the *air*. And there was news about the Vietnam War. That was before I was born."

And it was sure before I was born. Just like the Civil War. But I've read about both of them in history books.

"There were TV networks on that don't even exist anymore," Dad continued, "and it was missing some that have been around for years. What's going on?"

I still couldn't tell what had him so upset. It just looked like some kind of super-retro show, though even twentieth-century retro is pretty old-fashioned by now. Maybe it was just some new kind of wireless device.

"You say that seems strange to you?"

"Look . . ." My dad walked over and picked up a device with a numbered circle in the middle and a couple of speakers in the handset. He listened. "An old telephone. With a live signal."

That was a telephone? It was way too big!

"Television and phones haven't looked like this, or worked this way, in years. What is this?"

"How should a phone look?"

My dad took out his cell card and flipped it on. "Like this." The screen remained blank. "Nothing." Dad looked right into the motel guy's magnified eyes, and the motel guy looked right back. "What's going on?"

"My name is Andrew Jackson Williams," he said, offering his hand, "and I'm pestered by visions. Would you and your boy care to join me for dinner?"

● ● ●

A.J., as he liked to be called, grilled up a couple hamburgers for himself and Dad, and I was a little surprised, since real cow beef usually cost so much. But Dad enjoyed it. I'd never gotten used to the taste, so instead I had a cheese sandwich.

A.J. told us he used to be the preacher at the First Church in Vinita. "But I couldn't keep doing it," he said. "I had visions, and when I talked about them up in the pulpit, people got a little"—he looked around, as if someone else might be listening—"edgy."

"What kind of visions?" Dad asked, happily eating what was probably his first burger in years.

A.J. put his food down, then took a pen out of his pocket. He made a drawing on a napkin—a cloth napkin—and held it up. It was a circle.

"Time," he said, "doesn't really move in a straight line at all. It moves in and around everything, and them that know, know that everything really happens all at once. Or that everything that went before is still happening somewhere else. I'm putting it all down in the book I'm writing. I'm telling people that nothing ever goes away."

"What doesn't?" I asked. Sometimes I just don't know what grownups mean about anything.

"Personally," Dad said, putting the unfinished half of his burger down, "I'd like to give time a little rest. Maybe avoid it altogether, if I can."

"How are you going to do that?" A.J. asked.

"By going to California."

"Might work." He nodded, chewing thoughtfully. "It's worked for some." Now it was his turn to put down the burger. Then he pointed at me. "But it won't work for the boy. He's touched."

"Touched by what?"

"The hidden truth about time."

Now it wasn't just getting weird—it was getting scary. The conversation kind of died down after that, and after Dad took a couple more bites of his food, we went back to our room. The TV was still on. It showed a man running on a beach, being chased by a giant balloon.

As we stood there, there was a knock on the door. It was A.J.

"I don't mean to be inhospitable," he said, "but there's a break in the storm. This might be a good chance to move along to where you need to be."

My dad looked back at him. "I guess it might."

A.J. helped us get our stuff back in the car. "Hate to lose customers," he said, "but I'm pretty sure it's for the best." The full moon was reflecting off his glasses, but you could see how fierce and alive those eyes were.

"Let me pay you. . . ." Dad took out his wallet and held out a credit card.

"You probably know that your credit and your money won't work here."

"I probably do," my dad agreed. Then he did something that really surprised me; he took out a picture of my mom.

"I don't suppose . . ." And he let the question hang there for a while before finishing. "I don't suppose you've seen this woman anytime recently, have you?"

A.J. took the photo of Mom and squinted at it under the moon.

"I haven't seen anyone like that lately," he said at last.

"Lately?" Dad asked.

"It's been a long life," A.J. replied. Dad kept looking at him. "But I'll keep both eyes open for her."

Dad handed A.J. a slip of paper. "This is where we'll be in California," he said.

A.J. put it in his pocket without looking at it. "That's *where* you'll be," he said. "But *when* will you be there?"

"Just as soon as we can." And a minute later, Dad was steering the truck through the Oklahoma night, while I tried to stay awake in the seat next to him.

There was a lot I didn't understand about

what had happened, but there was one question I had to ask first. "Why did you show him Mom's picture?"

"Because, honey..." *Honey?* He hadn't called me *honey* in years. Since I was a kid. Now he was waving his hand at the windshield, indicating the night, the stars, and the moon. "I think your mother is still alive. Somewhere out there. Someplace."

"What do you mean?"

"I think the lab accident put her somewhere else in time, Eli. Some *when* else."

My stomach felt a little knotted up, like when you get bad news. But maybe this was good news. How come he never came out and told me any of this before?

"How?"

"There's a lot to explain. Can we talk about it in the morning, son?" He never called me *son* either. What was with him? "It's a long night, and I have a lot of driving to do. And you still have to get some sleep."

"That's not fair." I decided to stay up and keep asking questions, but somewhere in Kansas, I let my guard down and drifted off.

When I woke up, the sun was shining—it was almost scorching hot—and we were a thousand miles down the road, ready to eat a late breakfast in Arriba, Colorado.

Chapter Four

Eli: North of Joe DiMaggio
June 19, 2019 C.E.

Thirty hours after Colorado—I had pancakes there, even though it was near lunchtime—and more of my dad's high-speed driving (hydro-cell motors aren't usually loud, but he could really make ours scream), we arrived at the Valley of the Moon.

Like with most of our arrivals, we got there at night.

The only unusual thing that happened in that last part of the drive was that I finally got a message from Andy. We were driving through Nevada, and I was surfing around on my vidpad when I saw I had some new mail. I'd been expecting a package—a bunch of new Barnstormer character animations that Andy had made himself or gotten on his roamer, or maybe a clip of him talking to the screen. Instead, I was surprised to see that it was just a typed sentence:

How you doing?

It wasn't even his voice. Just the printed words.

"This whole trip has felt like the end of a game," I said, watching the words pop up on the vidpad as I composed a reply. "Like the way Barnstormers always have to flee town." It was on account of a low tolerance for monsters in most of the places they played. I was feeling a little bit on the run myself.

"But overall, not bad," I added to the message.

Looking at those short sentences made me feel farther from Andy, and from home, than the actual miles did.

And anyway, the big game I was getting sucked into was really just starting. Beginning with our arrival at Moonglow.

But what do you call a game that gets way too serious?

On the way out, since we were going to live near San Francisco, I read up on local baseball history. Turns out Joe DiMaggio came from there and played for an old minor-league team called the Seals, and of course Willie Mays played for the Giants in the old days, sixty or more years ago. Baseball historians say being a Giants fan is almost as hard as being a fan of the Cubs or Red Sox.

Maybe that's a bad omen, deliberately moving fifty miles north of such a run of hard luck. Apparently the person in our family who started Moonglow wrestled a lot with his luck, too.

It was some great-uncle of mine, Solomon, I think—in any case, a brother of my grand-dad, Silas Sands (and boy, am I glad my dad broke the "S" chain and didn't give me a name like Sam or Sylvester) — who tried to start the winery, with some money he made way back by investing in a company that made clunky old desktop computers that you couldn't even fold up.

I never met Solomon or my granddad, but when Dad was a kid, he spent part of a summer working at the winery before it went bust.

That's where the lucky streak started to wind down; a couple of plant diseases wiped out a lot of the grapes, and when the fruit recovered, my great-uncle found out nobody wanted to buy a wine called Moonglow, at least not one with a creepy picture of a glowing glass of green wine on the label.

That was my great-uncle again: He thought he was an artist, and insisted on designing the label himself.

So the winery sat there, and Solomon had some kids who grew up and eventually planned to use the land for a shopping center or something, but never got around to it. Both of them died, without kids of their own, so Moonglow wound up in my dad's hands, and sat there until the time that he needed to escape. When that tax bill came, reminding him of the winery's existence, I heard him laugh. It was the first time he laughed since Mom vanished.

The winery itself was kind of falling apart; the roof had holes, and water was getting inside.

Our first night there, we just took sleeping bags out of the car and found a dry spot on the wood floor in what used to be the tasting room.

On the morning of the third day, Dad drove to Sonoma in search of some basic roofing supplies. His idea was that he and I would fix up Moonglow and wait things out.

Which things?

I don't think he was sure. Life itself, maybe, so that no more bad stuff could happen to us.

I don't know why he thought that would work.

By the seventh day, we'd patched up several holes in the roof and polished the floors. We cleaned up a small dinette table and some chairs we'd found in an old employees' lunch-room and made that our kitchen.

There'd never been many employees—my dad, that summer, was one of the few—but there was a lunchroom.

The building sat next to a hill, and there were caves dug out of the side, which you entered from the winery. They were made of limestone and were used to store the wine at a cool temperature.

By the ninth day, I was really beginning to think that this wasn't just a phase my dad was going through, and maybe I could stay out of school for the whole rest of my life, since he hadn't gotten around to even *talking* about where I might want to go.

On the tenth day, a package arrived.

Now, Dad hadn't told anybody where we were going—well, nobody but A.J., but I'm not sure if that counted—but it wasn't neces-sarily a huge secret. We weren't trying to hide. I mean, I told Andy. And anyway, between stuffing a vidpad into your pocket and carrying a cell card, it's not like anyone was hard to locate.

But we weren't going out of our way to let anyone know where we were headed, either. We just locked up the house and drove straight out of Jersey.

And now here we were. Between our drive out and nailing tarpaper on the roof together, Dad and I were the closest we'd been since the accident. And then the package came.

From Mr. Howe.

There was no announcement, no preparation. An unmarked delivery truck just whizzed up our road, and a man stepped out, tapping a vidpad.

"You Mr. Sandusky?"

"I'm Sandusky Sands."

"Package. Sign here."

Dad looked at the pad, then up at him.

"Why?"

The man shrugged. "Suit yourself. I'm supposed to deliver it anyway." And with that, he opened the back and eased an enormous

wooden crate onto his hover-dolly, then low-
ered it onto the ground.

"You want this somewhere?"

Dad shrugged back. He was beginning to
slip back into his gray, blank sadness already.

The delivery man glided the crate over to
the tasting room, where we'd spent our first
night. When it still felt like camping and the
start of a new adventure.

After the truck hummed away, I went up to
look at the box. Dad hadn't moved.

I could see the label:

> DR. SANDUSKY SANDS
> MOONGLOW REMOTE LAB
> VALLEY OF THE MOON
> SONOMA CO., CALIFORNIA

On the top, instead of a return address, were
some familiar initials:

> *DARPA*

Dad didn't even open the crate. He just walked inside, sat down in a plastic chair in the old lunchroom, and started to cry.

Not for long, but just enough to scare me.

Not that I think guys shouldn't ever cry, or anything. But this was my dad.

Then suddenly he got up.

He walked to our truck and took out a crowbar and began popping slats off the box. Sure enough, there was a sphere generator inside. They wanted Dad to keep making the time spheres. And because he knew how to make them, no matter where he went, there wouldn't be any escape from Mr. Howe.

Now, instead of crying, Dad was smiling. Grownups' emotions are always so unpredictable.

"They'll never be able to make me use it," Dad said.

"Why not?" I asked.

"No WOMPERs," he replied.

"What are 'WOMPERs'?" They sounded like

some creatures from a Barnstormer game. Like a Frankenstein monster who could swing a mean bat.

"I'll tell you while we make dinner."

"Making dinner" was opening a couple cans of spaghetti and uncorking some wine. Well, Dad had the wine, and I had some chocolate rice milk. Sandusky had found a few cases of unopened Moonglow wine a couple days back and, for the first time, decided to crack open a bottle.

He was feeling pretty good again, all things considered, and told me about WOMPERs between bites of noodles and tomato sauce.

"WOMPERs stands for 'Wide Orbital Massless ParticlE Reversers,'" Dad said, writing it out on the side of a wine label so I could see where the capital letters fell to make up its nickname.

"They've only been recently discovered, in the farthest parts of space. The *oldest* parts. We theorized about them, but couldn't prove they really existed. We thought they were only around for a little while after the big bang, then disappeared."

"Why?"

"It takes too much concentrated energy to make a WOMPER. And the universe has been spreading itself pretty thin lately."

"What's a WOMPER do?"

My dad must've been excited by me asking all these questions. I usually left the science to him and Mom.

"If it passes through an electron or a proton, it reverses the charge. It can do this so rapidly that around any concentration — any buildup — of matter, it acts almost like an agitator in a washing machine." He was holding up his hand and waving it back and forth. "It does even stranger things to a positron."

"You mean the positrons you use for the time spheres?"

Those were the backward-traveling particles Dad used as the "fuel" for his, well, his time machines. Though he hates it when they're called that.

"Right. Since a positron is already a reversed particle — a backward electron — when it's hit by a WOMPER, the positron's properties are speeded up, made more intense. It blasts backward through time faster, with more energy."

"They make your time spheres stronger?"

"Exactly."

"So if you had some WOMPERs . . ."

"That's what Mr. Howe thought. Get some WOMPERs and rev these time spheres up. Make them work at warp speed."

"Would it?"

"We don't have to worry. WOMPERs don't occur naturally on Earth, or anywhere near it. Mr. Howe was able to get some once, but I don't think we'll be seeing any more of them in our lifetime."

He grew quiet again, then had some more spaghetti and some more red wine. Afterward, we bundled up in our sleeping bags and got the last good night's sleep we were going to have in a very long time.

If not forever.

Chapter Five

Eli: WOMPERs and Wolf House
June 30, 2019 C.E.

The next day, more men arrived. Some of them belonged to a power crew, and got heavy-duty electrical lines up and running to Moonglow by midafternoon.

I asked them where all the extra power was coming from.

"It's been arranged," one of them said. They didn't ask us to sign anything.

Dad and I took a walk while they worked. He didn't want to be near them. That was the first time we discovered Wolf House. Dad read the plaque about the writer, Jack London.

My dad stood and looked at the ruins of the house. "Imagine everything you love going up in smoke like that."

When we got back from the walk, Mr. Howe was waiting for us.

He just sat near the front door of Moon-glow, smiling again, this time like some out-of-town cousin who gets to your house early and waits around for you to let him in.

Next to him, by his feet, was a green box. Made out of metal.

"Sunny California," Mr. Howe said. "At least, when it isn't raining. Good for you." He stood up and held out the box. "Housewarming present."

Dad just looked at him.

"I suppose we shouldn't be surprised to see you," I said. Somebody had to say something. I pointed to the box. "What's in there?"

"Top secret, son," Mr. Howe said, winking at me. I *wasn't* his son.

"I'm done with secrets," Dad said.

"Not these secrets," Mr. Howe replied confidently. "Wait till you hear what they are." He leaned over and whispered in Dad's ear.

"WOMPERs?" my dad said out loud.

"You have WOMPERs? I thought they didn't occur on Earth," I added, looking at Mr. Howe suspiciously. He looked at me, then back at Dad. "Do you tell him *everything*?"

"The fact is, I haven't told him everything." Dad looked at me. "We used WOMPERs back in the lab at Princeton. They did supercharge the time sphere. And that's what caused the explosion."

"The one Mom was in?"

"Yeah." He was sounding far away again.

Then he turned to Mr. Howe. "You already cost me my wife. I'm done with your experiments. I don't care how many old space rocks you find."

"These aren't from space rocks. We have an almost limitless supply now. Thanks to nano-technology!"

I couldn't understand what he was saying. "Nano—what?"

"Nanotechnology." Dad repeated the word, looking at Mr. Howe, and looking a bit scared. "It's when you build things, Eli, molecule by molecule. A way to engineer living machines, even new life forms."

"We have a nanotechnology project at DARPA, too. Didn't I tell you? We don't concentrate only on time travel."

"But a WOMPER isn't a molecule. It's not even an atom." Dad was giving Mr. Howe his don't-lie-to-me look.

"We can make WOMPERs from other particles now. Call it . . . hyper-nanotechnology. It's not easy . . . but we can do it. There's nothing holding you back now." Mr. Howe thrust the box at my dad again. "Compliments of the house."

"Nothing holding me back, except my disgust for you."

Dad took me by the arm, stomped into the winery, and slammed the door.

I'm not sure how long we stood there blinking at the soldiers who were already inside.

At some point, I became aware the front door was opening and Mr. Howe was letting himself in. For some reason, he started speaking to me.

"Your dad's got to do it, Eli. Before somebody else does. Somebody who might not be working for *us*. Besides, it's *his* experiment."

"Don't look at me."

Over the next few days, Mr. Howe kept showing up with different squads of men. Not soldiers, though there always seemed to be a couple of those around to "guard" the place. And keep an eye on Dad and me.

These new guys, Mr. Howe would introduce as "fellow scientists." When it became clear they were trying to set up a kind of WOMPER reaction in the time sphere, Dad, who'd been successfully ignoring them the whole time, finally marched into the tasting room.

"I'll do it."

We all looked at him.

"I'll do it," Dad said again. "You'll just kill everybody."

Mr. Howe smiled.

As Dad worked, he talked. "Don't you worry about what the neighbors might think out here?"

"Don't worry," Mr. Howe said. "We bought up every house and ranch in a two-mile radius. Even took over that old park and closed it down." Which meant Wolf House and all the trails around it.

Dad just shook his head.

"It was national security, Sandusky. *National security.* We have to keep everybody safe."

"*We* didn't keep Margarite safe."

Safety was on Dad's mind, especially as he got close to creating the WOMPER reaction, so he agreed to let one of Mr. Howe's men take me down to San Francisco for a day while he brought the local spacetime field into a state of high excitement.

It worked. My dad didn't blow up the neighborhood. In fact, it worked so well that when I got back, something had already happened, causing everyone to stand around and just stare at the machine. The greenish glow of the time sphere was making their faces look even more pale than they already were.

Everyone was staring at something on the floor. Some kind of bundled paper.

"What's wrong?" I asked.

"The time sphere," my dad said. But it just sat there humming away, a perfectly normal time sphere from the looks of it.

"What?"

"It's a newspaper from 1937," Mr. Howe said. He was kneeling close to it, trying not to touch the little field of spacetime that Dad had created. "It was like it was just spit out from the past. It just *appeared* here."

"Like it was tossed through a hole," my dad added. "This time, there wasn't any explosion."

"Well, that's a good thing, right? I mean, you're still here."

Dad shook his head slowly. "This might be worse. We might've done something to the time stream. Things keep popping through."

"Like what?"

Dad was pointing. "That showed up right after the newspaper. It's an old—"

"Cool!"

I recognized the logo. I'd just seen one in a sports museum down in the city: the San Francisco Seals. I was considering making up a new Barnstormer squad called the Seals.

My first thought was, *Wow, if this was from the thirties, then maybe this was Joe DiMaggio's actual baseball cap from when he was a Seal!* Without thinking about it, I reached in to take a closer look—"Eli, no!"—violating every rule my dad had ever given me about being near the generator.

My hand went through the charged field to clutch the cap, and I could feel the jolt run up my arm. My whole body felt like Play-Doh being mashed around.

Somebody was screaming my name, and I think I screamed back, right before everything went black. And then exploded into color.

The colors stayed. But now I was sitting next to a dinosaur.

Chapter Six

Clyne: Homework
Final Class Project: 10,271 S.E.

Find an alternate Earth to visit and report on Saurian culture
there. Summarize your experience, and be sure to answer
the questions below. Remember, you will get history, social
studies, and science credits for this project, and the final
score will help determine your herd placement when you
leave middle school for the upper grades. Good luck!

THE QUESTIONS:

1. Where did you go?
2. Were the Saurians on the other Earth helpful?
   Why or why not?
3. How was this culture different from your own?
   Describe.

EXTRA CREDIT:

4. Would you recommend this reality to
   other students?

1. *Where did you go?*

As our science books teach, the Fifth Dimension is that passageway that connects different universes and different times to each other. My first trip through the Fifth Dimension, like that of most Saurians my age, was scheduled so I could finish my science research for graduation. I'd been told what to expect: It's as though you're moving through a kaleidoscope full of colors, sometimes traveling in slow motion. You feel like you're surrounded by warm mud, a nestling back in the egg, yet the egg is cracking at the same time, shaken apart at top speed.

I was moving through the Fifth Dimension, thinking about the various Earths described in our alternate history and geography texts, and wondering which one I should choose. There were the other known Saurian worlds such as Earth Fanda Rex, ruled by the child king, Fanda, and Earth Hydro, that planet covered almost entirely by water and populated by swimming beings who engage routinely in aquatic competitions and mermaid-themed costume balls.

But these Earths have been reported on in other classes, and I think one of my nest-mates even did his middle-school project on Fanda Rex, so maybe it's just as well things worked out the way they did.

Here's what happened: I was in my time-ship, charting a course toward one of the known alternate Earths, moving through the crosscur-rents of the Fifth Dimension, when all of a sud-den there appeared in the seat next to me a boy.

The boy was a growing hatchling like me. But he had skin that was monocolored and odd fur on top of his head, and he wasn't really any type or species of advanced Saurian at all. When I figured out what he was, I was as shocked as you will be when you read my answer to ques-tion two. But first let me tell you *where* I went.

I call it Earth Orange, because that is where I discovered you can taste colors! There, the color orange can be found in a sweet fruit tast-ing like a bright afternoon, though it can be hard on the Saurian stomach. The planet also reminds me of the orange lava that flows from our volcanoes. Not only in color but also because things always seem to be in danger of blowing up, exploding, or otherwise falling apart on this version of Earth.

The actual colors of this Earth, by the way, are similar to the blues, greens, browns, and yellows of our own planet. But I'm calling it Earth Orange because I want to, and because I get to. As far as I know, I discovered it. It's not mentioned in any of our texts or histories or on our maps.

Do I get extra credit for that?

You might well ask how I got pulled into an altogether undiscovered Earth. It turns out, I began my field trip at precisely the same moment three of their people were discovering the basic principles of time travel. On their Earth, they thought they belonged to "different" times, but as we Saurians know, time bends. They were actually working on opposite sides of a curve.

Or maybe different sides of a triangle. I

entered the Fifth Dimension at precisely the moment a female, Hypatia, who comes from the city Alexandria, and two males, Sandusky and Eli the Boy, who come from Valley of the Moon, solved the first basic step of rendering light into its component parts. Just as their own signals sparked through the Fifth Dimension toward each other, I entered the time stream in the ship I checked out from the school supply room.

At that precise instant, we were all fused together. Separate Earths, separate times, but suddenly a single destiny — that was how the moment was structured. We were like Saurians making a triple-jump move over each other's cranio-tops on the field of battle during a par-ticularly tail-curling game of Cacklaw — a move that can never be taken back.

The reason this Earth was unknown before was because no one on it had deduced how to time-travel. Until now. They aren't aware of the alternate Earths that surround them in multiple dimensions. On their planet, many act as if all truth and reality were immediately apparent. And easily known.

But as we know, the universe is more like a Cacklaw field than anything else, with its nooks, crannies, confusions, and unexpected connections.

The arrival of the Eli boy in my time-ship was proof of that. He appeared quite suddenly, and he was frightened—he had no idea where we were.

After his first long scream, he spoke. My lingo-spot took a moment to adjust. He spoke a kind of crude, guttural language filled with long, wheezy breathing sounds like *heeee* and *ahhh* and *wehhh,* with occasional tongue clicking thrown in to stop all the gasping. But at last some sense was made of all the noise.

"Where am I?"

"What are you?" I thought that was a reasonable question, since he was in my vessel. But he just stared at me as if I was speaking with a mouth full of petrified eggshells. Which, from his standpoint, I was. He couldn't understand me. I peeled off a little of my lingo-spot and dabbed it behind his ear. I hoped that, because of its plasmechanical properties, the substance would adapt to my guest's nervous system and biology in short order so that we could converse.

The boy looked scared when I reached out to him. "Don't be afraid. I'm just out on a field trip."

"I can understand you," he said, staring at me in disbelief. "But you're a dinosaur! Where is this? What's happening?"

A *dinosaur.* That's what we'd be called on Earth Orange. "You're in my vessel!" I told him. "I'm supposed to be doing schoolwork. We're in the Fifth Dimension, moving through time."

"Time . . ." He looked a little nauseous, then stared at a piece of blue cloth in his hands. I would later learn to call it a "cap." For now, he was transfixed by it. "Oh, no," he went on. "The Wompers." I still have not found out who the Wompers are.

Meanwhile, as we found out later, Hypatia, perhaps the senior female in her city of great learning, was creating a time beacon that was pulling us toward her, and toward the light-house—just like a water-ship heading for a beacon.

"Where are we going?" the boy asked.

I looked at my chrono-compass, which was spinning around wildly. Perhaps things hadn't stopped going wrong on this field trip after all. "I have no idea. You've upset all the controls."

"How come I understand you?"

I tapped the side of my head to indicate the lingo-spot. "School supplies."

2. Were the Saurians on the other Earth helpful? Why or why not?

There are *no* living Saurians on Earth Orange! Scanners do show traces of one or two "dino-saurs"—evolutionary cousins of ours—in a lake called Ness in a region called Scotland, and a couple of other places. But that's it.

There are no living Saurian *species*. By and large, they all became . . . extinct!

I expect I will lose points for this answer, as if I stayed home and made all this up, rather than going on my trip and doing actual research, but it's true. I shudder at the thought of a planet without Saurian culture, too. But I am attaching several history texts—translated from the rough languages of their planet—to show what they believe to be the truth: That one time, long ago, a comet collided with their Earth, causing a disaster that stopped Saurian evolution completely, like a dragonfly hitting a tar pit.

It's horrible to think about, and maybe it's just a crazy local myth. But could this event correspond to the same comet sighting in our own prehistory—and the prehistories of several other parallel Saurian Earths?—the nest-tale of the Great Sky Hammer? It was said to be a near miss with some kind of asteroid.

You will have a harder time believing what happened after this presumed extinction, though

I have digitized much visual and aural evidence and attached it to this homework. I hope to prove my thesis that on Earth Orange, in the absence of Saurians, *mammals* evolved.

Yes, mammals! Those little ratlike creatures who scamper around the feet of the more advanced Saurian species have grown here into all sorts of exotic creatures who roar, growl, beat their chests, walk around on two legs, and use all kinds of tools. Their records show that, like mammals everywhere, they also engage in the high-risk "live birth" of their young, as opposed to hatching from the vastly safer egg-and-nest method.

Eli the Boy was one such mammal. His species call themselves *Homo sapiens,* because they all presume they can think. They *do* have many languages. But they are always making trouble for each other and lighting many fires.

That said, I must add the most surprising thing of all: This Eli the Boy, this young mammal, has become my friend. As has Thea the Girl—born of Hypatia, the time scholar from

Alexandria—whom the boy and I would soon meet.

They were helpful because they trusted me and wound up defending me, despite our having just met. Like two leaf-eaters assisting a stranger in a roomful of carnivores—before knowing which I was.

I realize such closeness breaks all the basic rules about field-trip safety.

One thing about Earth Orange: It never runs out of ways to surprise you.

Chapter Seven

Eli: The Lighthouse
415 C.E.

I'd become unstuck, unglued in time. Tangled
in it.

Thanks to my dad's experiments, and Mr.
Howe's WOMPERs, I wasn't going to move
straight through from the beginning of my life
to the end of it, like everybody else. I was
going to be twirled around in time and history,
like a smoothie in a great big cosmic blender.

Strange things happen when you zigzag
through time like that. First, you go into the
Fifth Dimension, where it's much harder to tell
the difference between time and space, or when

and where. Or even who and what—you're not quite sure, when you're there, where *you* end and the rest of everything else begins. In the Fifth Dimension, things kind of *flow*. . . .

Time gets stretched out. And somehow, in some part of your brain, when you land in a ship next to a talking dinosaur, who turns out to be about your age in dinosaur years, you're not that surprised.

And when the time-ship journey seems to be taking a while, like a cross-country drive with your father, you get to know the dinosaur boy. After all, you're not going anywhere else. Yet.

His name is Clyne, and he was doing some kind of science project for his school. Apparently, by landing in his ship, I'd messed up all his careful calculations, and now his trip was ruined, because he didn't know where he was headed.

As it turned out, he was headed for ancient Alexandria, in the year 415. And so was I.

Judging from the sun, we arrived around noon.

We first appeared hovering over a giant lighthouse in the harbor. Now, arriving in a round, metallic ship in full daylight isn't exactly the way to slip in somewhere without being noticed. On top of that, there was a beam of rainbow-colored light pouring out of the tower, directly hitting Clyne's ship.

Making us even more obvious than we already were.

There was a big crowd of people around the lighthouse already, but whatever they were there for, they stopped doing it to stare at us.

Clyne looked through the glass at the people below. I was squinting because the rainbow beam was so bright.

"Mammal dance! *Tchkkk-tchkk-kk!*" Clyne said excitedly. He'd already taken off his lingo-spot in the ship, because after we'd been talking awhile, he said human speech seemed pretty simple, and if he learned it on his own, he could maybe fulfill some language require-ment at his school.

I decided to keep my lingo-spot on. There

was little chance I was going to learn to speak Lizard anytime soon. With or without the tongue-clicking.

As for what Clyne described as a "dance"— he was still figuring out which words go with which situations—to me it just looked like people standing still with their jaws open.

They were dressed in robes or tunics and wore sandals with lots of lacing. Their faces looked pretty sunburned, like maybe they spent a lot of time outdoors. This particular group all seemed to be holding rocks or clubs, and I thought I saw a drawn sword or two.

It didn't look like they'd come to dance.

Clyne checked some controls. "Cabin air good. Outside breathable." He tapped some gauges, then tapped them again. "Chrono-compass still unworking."

He stared, and tapped one more time. Then he turned to look at me with those big, round lizard eyes and shrugged. "Stuck in this present until fix-up. But where-when are we?" He looked through the glass. "Mammals below, on two legs, somewhat advanced, have streets, buildings, boats, and wagons." He turned back to me, still fairly cheerful. "Probably your planet! *Kkzht!* Let's look."

The speckled glass of Clyne's time-vessel slithered open along each side—I didn't even know there were windows in it.

Clyne stuck his head out.

They weren't silent anymore; you could hear them shouting. The lingo-spot let me understand them. "Devil!" someone screamed. "Demon!"

I heard a couple *thunks* against the side of the ship. Someone from down below was hitting us with rocks. They must've had a pretty good arm. Too bad for them baseball hadn't been invented yet.

Then my eye caught something else. We were hovering near the top of the lighthouse, and as the rainbow-colored beam moved away from us, I could see a girl, about my age, also wearing a robe, with dark hair around her shoulders. She was leaning out of one of the archways in the top of the tower, staring at our ship.

And now she was staring at me.

I didn't know what else to do. Through the open window, I waved.

Instead of waving in reply, she looked startled and stepped back. I guess I couldn't blame her.

Then she was joined at the railing by an older woman, who looked a little bit like her. Thick brown hair just kind of flowed around her face. Her mother?

The woman was shouting at us. At me.

Sometimes, when the lingo-spot was working hard, there'd be a tingle, and the slightest delay, like listening to an announcer in a ballpark.

"Where are you from?" she was asking.

"I'm from New Jersey!" I yelled back. "And the Valley of the Moon!"

I don't think they understood me.

It didn't matter, because my part of the conversation ended when a rock hit me on the forehead. It knocked me back into the ship, making me dizzier than even time travel does.

I touched my head and saw I was bleeding a little bit. I crouched and peeked out through another part of Clyne's ship—it was made from some kind of transparent metal, which we don't have on Earth—and saw one guy who'd actually climbed a few yards up the side of the tower.

He had a beard and long hair and eyes that seemed to pierce you from a mile away. His robes were brown and kind of scraggly, and he was shaking his fist at us.

I think the rock came from him.

"Maybe mammals aren't dancing," Clyne decided. He pulled the ship away from the lighthouse. "Yet both of us stuck in this 'now' until compass is fixed. Need to land—*k'ingg!*—and rethink studies."

We floated over the city of Alexandria: There were spires, stone boulevards, pillars, arches, and huge statues of men and warriors along the roadways. Also, a few statues of half-men or half-women. The other half would be animal—like a guy with a bird's head or something.

I wonder if they thought Clyne was like one of those statues come to life.

He was still looking for a place to land. Up ahead, we saw a wide clearing, mostly grass, with some bushes, in the middle of a huge complex of buildings. Like a palace courtyard turned into a giant park.

Clyne steered the ship toward it, hovered, landed. As we came down, we could see a couple people scurrying away.

The ship hit with a bump, and I stepped out. I reached down to put the Seals cap on my head . . . and felt my body tingling again. The colors of the Fifth Dimension swirled in front of me and I nearly passed out. . . .

"Boy sick?" It was Clyne, leaning over me, waving the hat in front of my face like a fan. "Time-stretching does that."

I started to wonder what was up with the cap.

I didn't wonder long, though. Coming up toward the ship, we had some new, curious visitors: a tiger, a pair of sauntering giraffes, and farther away, a rhino, stomping, head down, taking aim at the ship.

This wasn't just a courtyard. It was a zoo. And we'd landed in the middle of it.

Chapter Eight

Thea: Bazaar
415 C.E.

My name is Thea, daughter of Hypatia, last librarian in the city of Alexandria, keeper of archives and records, seeker of truth. This is my record, and whoever reads this, know that I would not lie. A lizard man and a boy wizard really did come to my city, fly around the lighthouse, and escape from a rhinoceros.

And that was before we'd been properly introduced. But *proper* is the wrong word for this story.

Their ship came at the stroke of noon. I'd climbed the tower with my mother, who was preparing a demonstration for her lecture on "The Bending of Light and the Movement of Time."

With the sun at its zenith, she revealed a carefully placed row of crystal prisms she'd set up in front of the lighthouse mirror. Normally, that mirror is used at night, or during dense fog, when the flame of Pharos burns and is reflected and thrown far out to sea.

But now, the lighthouse threw instead a blazing rainbow, and within moments, the airship appeared.

"What's happening?" I asked Mother. There had always been whispered stories about ancient flying ships from distant lands, but I had never seen one before.

"The lighthouse signal seems to have drawn another kind of ship here. I wonder where it's from? Or, perhaps, *when* it's from? And if it's friendly." My mother looked at the rows of crystals. She'd spent months shaping them and calculating how to line them up. "I wonder if this was such a good idea."

I leaned out over the railing to get a closer look at the ship, and that's when I first saw the boy.

He was staring at me, too.

"Where are you from?" I shouted, but I'm not sure he understood me. He said something that sounded like "Neujarzii," but it made no sense.

Still, we might have shouted more questions, marveling at each other's strangeness, if "Brother" Tiberius hadn't hit him in the head with a rock.

Tiberius is friends with Cyril, the head of the church in our city. It used to be the Romans who ran the place were always mad at the Christians. Then the Christians began taking over, especially Cyril, and it was their turn to get mad at the Romans.

So the Christians began doing to everybody else what had been done to them.

Mother said, "People have long memories

here in Alexandria. And in a place with so many different names for God and heaven, that can be dangerous."

Perhaps the city is not so advanced after all.

Tiberius had been saying in public that Mother was a witch, because she lived alone—without a husband—and because she played music, knew both elemental and advanced science, and believed in Serapis.

Serapis is a god who dwells mostly in the underworld. They say he brings light and dark together and can heal both human and animal.

I don't know if he's real.

Nor, at that moment, did I care. The ship disappeared, heading off in the general direction of the Royal Quarter with its museum, zoo grounds, and library. And it didn't seem as though Serapis, or anybody, human or god, could get us safely out of that tower.

I wished that we were on the airship, too. Between the appearance of the boy wizard and his strange, lizard-like companion, Tiberius and his dozens of followers were convinced, utterly and forever, that Mother and I were witches of the most terrible sort. It didn't help that the lizard man resembled the snake-like parts of Serapis.

"If you leave now, we won't harm you!"

There was just one thing they did to witches.

Letting them go without harm was not it.

But Tiberius was shouting from below, suddenly claiming he was going to give us secure passage out of the lighthouse.

"Is it a trick, Mother?"

"It has to be," she replied. "But I don't know how else we're going to get out."

"Then we'll stay."

"Then we'll starve. Or they will get in eventually." Mother lifted my chin and smiled right into my eyes. "Don't worry. For all his ravings, Tiberius is right about one thing. Sometimes there is magic in the world. Maybe we can trick them, too."

She and I went down the seemingly endless stairs to the bottom and flung open the doors.

Tiberius and his mob were waiting. He smiled. "Witches. We only want you out of our midst. We've seen your trickery. It's too strong for us. Please. Just . . . go."

He gestured with his hand, and the crowd parted like a gate being swung open. We stepped through.

There was a long, narrow bridge running along the top of the seawall that controlled the flow of water into the harbor and connected Pharos to the mainland. The way across seemed clear. "We mean no harm to anyone," Mother said, looking directly at Tiberius. "We're interested in truth. And in what light can teach us."

"You're lecturing again, Hypatia. Leave here. Walk away, go back to your library, and be out of Alexandria by sunrise. Let the light teach you that."

Mother's shoulders sagged a little, and she turned away, putting an arm around my shoulder. "Come, sweet Thea."

"'Sweet Thea.'" That was Tiberius repeating the phrase, mocking us.

"Does sweet Thea have slow pox, too?" he went on. "Or is she protected by one of your charms?"

The slow pox epidemic was something else that was blamed on us. We were suspect because no one at the library had come down with it. In truth, I think the only "magic" we used was that we bathed regularly.

"We don't use charms." Mother still had her back to him.

"It's said witches never suffer from their own spells. If you caused the sickness, and we let you leave, perhaps you'd take the cure with you. We can't have that."

Suddenly a hand shoved me off the bridge, and I was engulfed by the warm green-blue of the Mediterranean. I recovered and swam back to the top. When I broke the surface, I could see my mother's face. "Swim!" she yelled at me. It was her hand that had pushed me. They were hauling her away.

"Swim!"

Her last words to her child.

But she also knew swimming would give me a better chance than running. I am a good swimmer—Mother used to call me Mermaid as a nickname—but, more important, I could now see Tiberius had the other end of the bridge blocked off by two fierce-looking men. He had never had any intention of letting us go.

I could swim back toward the necropolis. There was an underground tunnel there with an entryway near the harbor. It led back toward the library.

It might have been safer to travel underground, but speed was more important to me. I decided to swim for the docks and return to the library on foot, and, once there, I would get help. Besides, since the slow pox had broken out, there were a lot of unburied dead down in the catacombs. And I was in no mood to make my way past them in the dark.

As I swam away, an arrow whizzed past my nose, disappearing in the water.

An arrow!

Normally only palace guards carry bows and quivers. Who among Tiberius's men was shooting at me?

Tiberius's influence—and Cyril's—must have been growing among the guards themselves. I knew then there would be fewer and fewer safe places for me.

Another arrow skimmed by me. Swim, Mermaid!

A few minutes later, I pulled myself out of the water, up on the wooden pilings of the harbor, shivering and soaked. But I had very little time before Tiberius and his mob would catch up with me.

I hurried to the Gate of the Moon, the main entrance to the city from the harbor side, staying close to the city wall instead of the main boulevard. The fewer people who saw me, the better.

As I approached the Royal Quarter, I was surprised to see a few vendors still lined up by their stalls or selling trinkets from blankets.

Normally, you could buy everything and anything here—fruits, nuts, olives, smoked meats, fabric, and spices from far-off lands. You could find the services of a medic or a midwife, or get your fortune told.

Since the pox had come, however, the open-air bazaar was supposed to have been closed down. But people still have to eat. And to eat, some people still had to sell.

"Child, child . . ."

I recognized her. Her name was Sarai, one of the fortunetellers. She saw me shivering and took the shawl from around her shoulders to wrap around me.

"Thank you . . . ," I gasped.

Sarai handed me a piece of smoked fish. And then, looking around so as not to be seen, she slipped a small statue of Serapis into my hand. "For protection," she whispered.

But I hardly noticed. I was watching a griffin vulture fly by overhead. The only griffin vulture I knew about lived in a cage in the zoo.

How could he have gotten out?

In answer to my question, the animals roared; elephants were trumpeting, and you could hear human screams from the grounds-keepers. As this terrible music grew louder, the lizard man leaped over the mighty wall from the garden side and landed in front of me!

In his arms, he was holding the boy wizard.

Everyone in the bazaar was shouting, too, falling all over themselves to get away. Everyone except Sarai.

"*Who* are you?" I asked them.

The boy wizard spoke again in some strange tongue.

At that moment, Tiberius's mob rounded the corner. They stopped and pointed at the lizard man.

"Look at the creatures she commands! Can there be any doubt she's a sorceress?" It wasn't Tiberius who spoke, but someone stockier and beardless. Where was their brave leader now? "And that this sorceress should not be allowed to live?"

Somehow, the boy wizard and lizard man

knew what was being said. They looked at each other, then at me.

The boy nodded, and the lizard man put him down. Then picked me up.

I was still shivering.

The small Serapis talisman fell out of my hand. The boy bent down, perhaps to give it back to me.

But by now the lizard was holding me tight and began bounding away on powerful legs.

Tiberius's followers tried to give chase but could not keep up. Angry and exhausted, they turned their attention to the boy.

The last glimpse I had was of the boy hopelessly surrounded.

Until he put on some kind of soft helmet — and disappeared.

Chapter Nine

Eli: DARPA
August 2, 2019 C.E.

The van is making that vibrating sound, like we're going over a bridge. I bet we're heading back toward San Francisco. But with blacked-out windows, it's hard to tell for sure.

Mr. Howe is sitting on the seat next to me, along with a couple of his uniformed goons. I guess they're trying to figure out what to do with me, now that they know I'm unstuck in time.

I've been back awhile. I've told them a little about Alexandria, what I remember. I described the lighthouse. And the zoo. I haven't told them about Clyne, though. Or his ship. They'd probably just think I'm crazy, which might make the situation worse. Besides, I don't know if I *want* them to know about Clyne. That might be dangerous for him.

Anyway, why should I trust them? They still haven't told me where my dad is. I nearly made it all the way to Wolf House yesterday, but no sign of Dad anywhere. "I guess you'll just have to voluntarily stay inside from now on," was Mr. Howe's only comment when they brought me back.

But I don't get to "voluntarily" use a vidpad, or a roam box here in the van. So I can't do any Barnstorming. So many free choices and all for my own good.

"Devices like that can be tracked electronically. We can't take any chances." That's Mr. Howe again, explaining for about the twentyhundredth time why I have to be bored out of my skull.

Don't they know I need something to

distract me? When you've been time-traveling . . . you're left kind of . . . *haunted* by things. Like the colors and eerie quiet of the Fifth Dimension. Or the fact that I left a couple people behind in Alexandria who were in big trouble . . . a week ago. And who knows what shape they're in now?

"Here. Use these to pass the time. On us." Mr. Howe hands me a pack of baseball cards. I don't know why they still call them cards. Tradition, I guess. They're more like small circuit boards, with moving holograms on the front.

Howe's given me a "Hall Heroes" pack— in other words, 'grams of players recently drafted into the Hall of Fame. I got a Barry Bonds, a Ken Griffey Jr., and a Mark McGwire. Not bad. There's Bonds, hitting number 700 into the same bay I'm probably being driven over right now. There's McGwire, breaking the single-season home run record, which Bonds would break again.

I've seen old cards in collectors' shops, of

course. They don't move at all. With the 'grams, you get to watch a bunch of career highlights over and over again, so you don't get bored quite as fast.

Now if I can just imagine Barry Bonds as a werewolf, I'll have a Barnstormer game.

They woke me up this morning to come here. I'd been dreaming again. I keep seeing the colors spilling out from the lighthouse. And the rhino charging the time-ship. That seems to be another problem with time travel—you get less and less sure where your dreams leave off and your actual life begins.

My dad still wasn't anywhere around. Mr. Howe said he would take me to meet him.

"Where is he?" I asked.

"We can't tell you. But you need to come with us."

"Why? Are you taking me to him?"

"It's only an hour's drive," he said. But that didn't answer my question.

He tried to give me what he thought was a

reassuring smile, but it didn't sit right on his face. Instead, he looked like someone waking up from surgery, when the knockout gas hasn't quite worn off. Like the smile came from outside him and wasn't an expression he could make on his own.

Now we seem to be going down, driving on a long ramp, or in an echoey tunnel. The windows may be blacked out, but you can still feel slopes. And hear sound.

We stop and the sliding door is flung open. More uniformed guys are standing around. I step out, and the air feels damp. It's some kind of giant underground garage with rows of lights way overhead. Lots of cement. Pipes running along the walls. We're walking toward what seems like a complex of offices behind a large Plexiglas window. Why put in a window? What's so great about a view of a dark, damp cement garage?

I see some more guys in DARPA jumpsuits running around. "Where are we?"

"We can't really tell you," Mr. Howe tells me, and I'm starting to wonder why I bother asking any questions at all.

"It's an old BART tunnel," a voice says. "But since the train doesn't come through here anymore, it's like our own private station."

It's a woman's voice. I turn, and she's stepping out of a private train that whooshed in silently from one of the dark tubes. She's in a blue business suit, and her hair is blond, streaked with gray. She wears it loose. When *she* smiles, at least, it seems more real than when Mr. Howe tries it. "They had to build several different subway tunnels after the last earthquake. This was one of the old ones they left behind. A real fixer-upper. But office space is so expensive aboveground. This was a steal."

I stare at her a moment. She seems so different from Mr. Howe that I'm beginning to think it was less strange running into a dinosaur. "Who are you?"

She shrugs. "Number Thirty." She gives me

the smile again, like she has warm cookies for me, but of course she doesn't.

"That's your name?"

She points to my baseball cards. "That was Griffey's number. It'll be my name for today." Two men in dark blue suits step out of the train car, and the shadows, to stand next to her. "And we'll call these two Twenty-Five."

I look back at the cards: Both Bonds and McGwire wore number twenty-five. I consider asking Mr. Howe something, and decide it'd be useless. Instead, I say to Number Thirty, "Don't tell me you people brought me this far for some kind of Barnstormer game."

"Me and the two Twenty-Fives, here. We're the Referees."

"Baseball has umpires."

"Well, we're known here as Referees. We kind of do what the Supreme Court does. Except they make public decisions."

She lets that hang there.

"And you make secret ones?"

"Private ones. For DARPA, and other agencies. When things happen that there aren't any rules for yet. We help make up those rules."

"But then who gets to know what they are?"

She doesn't answer, turning to Mr. Howe instead. "You're right. He is a smart boy." Then she leans in close to me. "Come on, Eli Sands. Let's find out what we should do with you. And whether there's any chance of getting your mother back."

She turns and walks toward the Plexiglas office, with the Twenty-Fives in tow. She's whistling a little song—from a Disney movie, I think, but I've been too old for those since at least 2015. It's an ancient one, about being happy while you work. I wonder how much she really cares about my mom.

Soon, I'm in a soft, fancy chair—like the kind you might find on an airplane—looking up at a blank white wall. The wall brightens and shimmers into life with a series of 3-D images.

There's a picture of Andrew Jackson

Williams, standing in front of the CABIN CREEK sign—except there's no motel on that corner now. The sign says CABIN CREEK CLEANERS. But Dad and I were just there in June.

And how did they find out, anyway? Were they following us?

"This is from the *Daily Oklahoman* site. Headlines from a few days ago. A town named Vinita. You've heard of it?"

I don't say anything.

Number Thirty keeps talking. "It's a man named Andrew Jackson Williams. He wrote a book called *The Time Problem*. About time travel. Have you heard of *that*?"

"No."

"No, we didn't think so. It was published in 1969. The hippies back then really liked the book. They thought it was 'far-out' and 'cosmic.' But A.J. never really liked hippies."

"What's a hippie?" I ask.

"Never mind." Now it's Mr. Howe's turn. I guess the Twenty-Fives are just going to keep quiet. "The point is, Eli, Andrew Jackson

Williams died in 1969, too. Right after his book came out."

It's a good thing everyone's looking at the wall screen, and not my face. I'm feeling pretty nervous. "He died?"

"Apparently. In the middle of a thunderstorm. According to the news stories we could find. Except that suddenly, he's been seen again all over his hometown of Vinita."

More shots of him go by, posing with a vidpad — like it's some strange object from space — and standing in front of a church, giving a lecture. You can tell all the pictures are recent.

"Is he a ghost?"

"He doesn't seem to think so. He claims that during the storm, he just walked out of the motel he owned, and when the storm broke, here he is, fifty years later." There's another picture of him in front of the cleaners. There's still no motel.

"Mr. Williams says it has to do with a sudden disturbance in time. Though when local authorities asked him about it, he said they'd have to read his book." Mr. Howe shrugged. "Except the book's been out of print for nearly fifty years."

There's a *thunk* as a copy lands on the table near me. Even in the dark, I can see it's old and beat-up. The whole thing is printed on paper. "We've read it," Howe added. "It didn't answer any of *our* questions."

"Look at this." Now it's Thirty's turn again. On the wall screen, a group of airline passengers stand around a busy airport terminal, looking confused and worried like they could all use a nap.

"This just happened yesterday," she says. "A flight from L.A. to New York. It's supposed to take three and a half hours, nonstop."

"Yeah?"

"According to everybody's watches, and every clock we could check, and every way we could measure . . . it took fifteen minutes."

"What?"

"That's right. They left Los Angeles, and before they had time to finish hearing about the inflatable life rafts in case of emergency, they were over Manhattan. This one we've kept out of the news. For now. The crew and passengers are still being debriefed in a hotel."

"They get a hotel? And I'm stuck in a tunnel?" No one's laughing, and I'm not sure I meant it as a joke. "So what does 'debriefed' mean?"

"It means held against their will." That was a new voice. Dad's.

He's come in the room and is standing in the back. "Daddy!"

I haven't called him that in about five years. Since around the time I stopped watching Disney movies.

I can feel my cheeks get a little red, then he walks up and hugs me and I don't care . . . except he's wearing latex gloves, so it feels a little funny.

"I'm sorry, buddy, but I came down here

late last night. Mr. Howe told you this morning, right?"

"No."

We both try to glare at Mr. Howe, but he just won't feel embarrassed about anything. "I wasn't sure you'd be finished," he claimed. "I didn't want to promise the boy he'd see you if you weren't going to be here. I didn't want to upset him."

There are times when Mr. Howe makes me want to barf.

"You should have told me you were leaving, Dad." I let go of him so I can stand back and look him in the eyes.

"Eli, we discovered something . . . and I didn't want to get your hopes up too much. I was in a sealed room farther down the tunnel. You couldn't have come in there, anyway."

I realize Dad is dressed in a special jumpsuit, too, like some of the DARPA guys. He doesn't look right in the uniform.

"What's going on?"

Dad peels off the gloves and takes a small

vidpad out of his pocket. "We just scanned these in. Nobody can touch it directly, of course. We had to be very careful."

They were pages from the old *San Francisco Chronicle* that popped up in his lab at the same time the baseball cap did.

"Funny things have been going on with time, Eli."

"You think I don't know that?" Then I lower my voice so only he can hear. *"Are you talking about the motel we stopped at?"*

"No. Look." He scans through the news-paper pages, then stops, enlarging an article about an orchestra playing in San Francisco back in 1937.

There's a picture of one of the flute players looking toward the camera. Margarite Sands. My mom.

Chapter Ten

Clyne: The Rhino and the Time-Vessel

Final Class Project: 10,271 S.E.

3. How was this culture different from your own? Describe.

Since I've already described this planet as being dominated by evolved mammals, I have, in a way, already answered the question. What could be more unusual than that? But you still may not believe me, and may even be thinking that when I get home, the school nurse should immediately prescribe a volcano cure for me to let me sweat out these bad visions. But our motto, as Saurians, has always been "Science is deep truth," and science is on my side here.

Even though the truth is that *everything* is different, and what we thought we knew about evolution has been turned into mush-fern stew.

For example, there are nearly as many types of mammal species as there are Saurians! Not just the two-legged, mostly sentient kind like Eli the Boy, or Thea, the daughter of the scholar Hypatia (and a scholar in her own right), but many other strange creatures with equally strange names: rhinos, monkeys, tigers. They have "birds," too. These birds even resemble our own winged Saurians.

I met many of these firsthand, when they tried to overrun my vessel in the middle of something called a "zoo." The human mammals evidently keep other mammals imprisoned, like the Ring of No Escape in Cacklaw. And, like Cacklaw, it's for entertainment. But not for a few mere sun-cycles as in our own sporting events, with the gates open after the game. No, these zoos are permanent. Does this mean, for mammals, that *their* games don't end? It seems more serious for the ones behind bars. I will continue to investigate.

My introduction to the culture, of course, was when Eli the Boy wound up in my ship as a result of a poorly plotted experiment on time dynamics. Their mature beings, called "grownups" or "adults," possess roughly the scientific knowledge of a Saurian in secondary studies. As a result of this rough science, my settings were thrown completely off.

We know from our own studies that certain beings can potentially act as "lightning poles," magnets if you will, for time energy — with the slightest disturbance in spacetime focused on and channeled through them. As the saying goes, "Some hatch differently." The boy is like that. Apparently, his unique reactions are triggered by the wearing of headgear, or a "cap."

As a living time particle himself, Eli the Boy was drawn to another time experiment in Alexandria, a place that was "ancient" for him, since it reached the height of its glory some sixteen hundred years before he was born. Thea's female parent, Hypatia, had retreated to a lighthouse after solving several equations about the composition of light and time, and how each measures and affects the other. She was trying to demonstrate the results for the whole city, perhaps because she thought some citizens might appreciate what would be a great forward stomp in mammalian knowledge.

Hypatia's experiment acted as a kind of homing beacon for us. Since I found myself back in a fairly normal, compressed atmosphere, I stuck my head out of the ship's portal to get a better view of our surroundings, and to bring the standard time-traveler's greeting to the crowd below: "A good time to meet!"

But I never got that far. They began throwing projectiles and chanting at us. Apparently, they were not fond of Hypatia or her experiments.

As the ship was still wobbly, Eli the Boy and I looked for a place to put down. When we found open space in this "zoo," we were attacked first by the rhino, and then by other creatures, who presumably thought, as had the humans, that their territory was being invaded.

After getting out of the ship, I just stood there transfixed, watching these amazing creatures come at us. The rhino might've speared me dead center in my abdo-bilious if Eli the Boy hadn't shoved me away. A rude gesture for a kind purpose.

In their own way, these Earth Orange animals are wondrous. Like creatures you might find in a hatchling's tale. But they also have appetites—and tempers.

"I think we made him mad," Eli the Boy said as the rhino turned around to face us again.

Now it was my turn to help. Holding the boy, I jumped to safety, hearing behind me the distressing *thud* of the rhino colliding with my ship. My leaping seemed to amaze the other humans scrambling for safety around us. Apparently, human legs are slow and spindly.

I leaped across the great grounds of these

Royal Quarters, over fountains, pillars, and arches, trying to keep ahead of the strange riot that was brewing between the interplay of mammals — the animals who were loose, and the various humans running from them in panic. Even in this confusion, I had time to notice that Alexandria, in all its pink, sandy tones, is very much like a Saurian city!

But our first task was getting to safety. So I cleared the walls, still holding on to Eli the Boy, thinking we'd be safe once we were away from all the stampedes.

Instead of tigers and lions, we found more humans. The angry mob had chased the girl up from the lighthouse and into the public market, where they had her surrounded. Then I saw Eli the Boy do an amazing thing.

After my appearance caught them off guard once more, Eli declined to continue our escape and instead released himself from my arms.

"Get her away from here," he instructed me.

Here I'd just arrived on their planet, and they were already getting me involved in their fights. This certainly wasn't a typical school assignment!

But I trusted Eli, and had a sense that the girl—for I didn't know her as Thea yet—could use a helping claw. I took her, and, as we jumped away, caught sight of something extraordinary:

Eli voluntarily put himself in danger, drawing the wrath of the mob, giving Thea and me a better chance to escape. Then he put his cap on and disappeared back into the Fifth Dimension.

Meanwhile, I took the girl and returned over the wall into the Royal Quarters, since the four-legged mammals suddenly seemed less dangerous than the two-legged ones.

I heard another distant *thump* as the rhino kept charging at my poor ship. The girl spoke to me, but in a tongue different from the boy. Apparently Earth Orange is so early in its development that it is still multilingual! I could see I would need the lingo-spot again to learn how to converse with her.

I had some of the plasmechanical substance in the emergency kit in my uniform, and I quickly applied some. She was pointing frantically toward some buildings on the edge of the great lawn, and I jumped in that direction.

After we landed, she turned to me. "Are you a lizard god? Or just a lizard man?"

I responded, but she couldn't understand me. I reached out to give her a lingo-spot, but she stepped back. I could understand her caution, but it would take me at least a few minutes to pick up some words in her language.

"Well," the girl said, "I suppose it doesn't matter who you are. Or what. Thank you for your help. You're in my city, Alexandria, now. And I'm afraid you've come at a very dangerous time.

"This is the library. We have all the knowledge in the known world here. My mother, Hypatia, is the head librarian, lecturer, and the city's principal mathematician. I am Thea. I have recently discovered a new star and am also finishing a rebuttal to Pythagoras. He claimed each number has a male or female personality, but he made too many of them masculine."

There was a pause after that, then she grew terribly sad. "I suppose none of that matters now. I saw them take her away." Then she did something strange: It involved water coming out of her eyes, which she eventually wiped off. After she regained her breath, she looked right at me—a look of amazing intelligence. "Whatever you are, you're in danger, too. No, Tiberius won't stop until everything he can't control, or doesn't understand, is destroyed. And he wouldn't even try to understand you."

"No," I said. It was my first word in her tongue. She looked surprised. But I still don't know if I meant "No, he won't understand," or just "No," as if I could personally stop what had already been set in motion.

It turned out none of us could. Not even Eli the Boy, when he returned to us through time mere minutes later.

Chapter Eleven

Eli: DARPA — The First Tunnel
August 2, 2019 C.E.

I keep looking at the picture of my mom. I don't think my dad knows what to say, either. He just looks sad, drained, and even weirdly amused, all at once. "She always wanted more time for her music," he says.

More time for her music? I get really impatient when grownups make bizarre jokes that only they understand. Especially in a situation where it makes more sense to be scared. "Well, is she all right?" I ask. "Does she still know who she is? Or where she really belongs?"

Dad adds a small shrug to his mixed-up expression. "No one knows, Eli. I wish I did. I'm sorry. I don't think anybody's ever been in a situation like this."

Mr. Howe comes over. "The world has never been in a situation like this, and we have to try to fix it." He turns to Thirty and the Twenty-Fives. "We have to fix this before it gets out of hand!" The Referees don't respond.

"Dad? Before what gets out of hand?"

Mr. Howe answers me before Dad can.

"Time! If time, in fact, really doesn't move in just one direction . . . if history can be rearranged behind our backs at a moment's notice . . . then everything we know could be changed"—he snaps his fingers—"like that. I mean, what if George Washington suddenly loses the Revolutionary War, and there's no America? Or for you, personally, one of your grandparents winds up married to somebody else, and you wink out of existence? Or worse, what if that happened to someone important? What then?"

"Who's deciding who's important, Howe? You? DARPA?" My dad is standing up now. "I mean, what if hydrogen bombs were never built? What about that?"

"What are you talking about now!?" Mr. Howe is sweaty and nervous, and turns back to the Referees. "What is he talking about now?"

Thirty looks at my dad. "What *are* you talking about?"

"It's just that there are some things about history we might be *better off* changing."

"We're not here to play God, gentlemen," Thirty says to both of them.

"Why not?" Mr. Howe snaps. Everyone stares at him. "I mean," he adds, "if the mission requires it."

Dad glares at him, getting more and more annoyed. "I think we need to remember the reason this is happening is that Mr. Howe kept pushing me to do the experiments before we knew where they would lead."

Howe stares at my dad. "You told me once,

Sandusky, that the part you loved best about your work was when something totally unexpected happened. You liked the surprise. Well, I'd say you got it."

"Dad," I say, loud enough so Mr. Howe can hear, "do you think you could both stop arguing? So we could figure out how to get Mom back?"

That actually shuts them up for a minute. Then Dad takes me by the shoulders. "In a way, that *is* what we're trying to figure out. They brought me down last night, Eli, to brief me on the situation, and to ask my permission."

"Permission for what?"

"They want to send you back to Alexandria."

Now it's my turn to shut up for a minute. I hear water dripping somewhere in the BART tunnel.

"Specifically, *Mr. Howe* wants to send you back." It's Thirty, speaking as the Twenty-Fives nod repeatedly. "It's our job, as Referees, to decide if he has a case."

"And then what?" I ask.

"We give the agency our approval to go ahead."

"You can't make him go against his will." My dad says it out loud, just as I'm thinking it.

"It's not just about trying to fix time and space anymore or even how to get Dr. Margarite Sands back to her family." Before any of us can ask Thirty what it *is* about, the wall shimmers back to life with more images from Vinita.

Mr. Howe jumps as though he hasn't seen these pictures before, either. Maybe DARPA is even keeping secrets from him.

The wall screen shows Andrew Jackson Williams and a bunch of other people being taken away by men in Thickskins—material that sticks to your real skin and protects it if you're in an area where there's something dangerous in the air. It covers your nose, too, and your eyes, but you can breathe and see through it. It makes people look like big, shiny bugs.

Only the government's supposed to have it. But I touched some once—when Dad brought some of the material home.

"There've been outbreaks in Vinita and a few other places. As we did with the airplane incident, we've kept them out of the news. But not much longer."

"Outbreaks of what?" I'm like Clyne with my questions.

"Slow pox. A disease that causes a slow withering of the nervous system. Usually irreversible. Toward the end, people are prone to violent outbursts. The last outbreak we know about was before the Middle Ages. Before the Black Plague, actually. In Alexandria, around the year four hundred." Thirty looks straight at me. "But we thought slow pox had been eradicated—or died out on its own—a couple of centuries back.

"Then early this morning . . . this." On the screen, there's a section of a tile mosaic, a kind of landscape, or cityscape. The colors are still amazingly vivid, and I recognize the buildings, and the pink-blue light on the water. "This is an artist's rendition of people fleeing a great fire in the library at Alexandria—done in tile about a hundred years or so after the actual event. It's usually on display in the British Museum, in London. But not today. This was first discovered—rather excitedly, I might add—by a child visiting the museum on a field trip."

The lower-right corner of the image has been enlarged. You can make out the robes and sandals on the people running from the blaze. There's a rhino stampeding by.

And then, coming out of the library behind them is . . . Clyne. I don't know how else to explain it. But it looks like Clyne. Running on his two legs, looking over what's basically his shoulder at the flames behind him.

Thirty doesn't know about Clyne. She has a different explanation.

"The two legs, the gray lizard-like skin, the big eyes. This might be a gray alien."

"What?"

"A gray alien. Look at the large head. Oh, don't be surprised, Eli. We're not alone in the universe. Mr. Howe can show you the reports sometime. By the way, Howe, does he know he's sworn to secrecy about all this?"

"Yes."

Well, I do now.

"Do you mean," Mr. Howe says slowly, "that an alien race is trying to invade us . . . by invading our history first?" He's worked himself up into a sweat.

"It's possible." Thirty stays calm. "The WOMPERs may have created a breach in spacetime around our whole planet. Everything we thought we knew about our history could be changed, or changing, with unimaginable consequences. Like ancient diseases reappearing as new plagues. And it's possible that other races, other beings, who already know how to travel in spacetime . . . are taking advantage of our predicament to *make* these things happen. A gray alien suddenly appears in a museum picture, when he wasn't there before, because he decides to surprise us by getting here about sixteen hundred years early."

Thirty sure seems satisfied with herself, getting all that figured out. I want to tell her it wasn't an alien, just a two-legged dinosaur. From a parallel Earth. And he's not invading. Or making anyone get sick. He's just trying to do his homework.

"And what do you think my son can do about any of this?" Dad is sweating, too.

"Alexandria seems to be one of the keys. He needs to go back there."

"And do what?" I ask.

"Find out what you can about treating slow pox. See if you find any aliens." That's Thirty's advice.

"Fix what's wrong." Mr. Howe is less helpful.

"I don't know how. I'm just a kid." Nobody seems to be listening to me. "And anyway, what if I just want to go back and find my mom?"

Dad gets his sad look back. "The truth is, Eli, we're not a hundred percent sure *where* you'll wind up. Or if you'll go anywhere at all. I've been running calculations, and I think since the WOMPER accident, your whole body is like a supercharged particle traveling backward in time."

"But I'm here now. I'm staying here. I'm not moving." I look around at all the grownup faces. "Right?"

A cart with a metal box on top is wheeled over to me. Mr. Howe puts on some Thick-skin gloves, opens the box, and takes out my Seals cap.

How did that get here?

"It's the baseball cap, Eli," Dad says. "For some reason, that's what carries the particular WOMPER charge that sets you off. Completes it. Turns you into a kind of giant positron."

"Just me? Can't someone else do it?"

Dad glares at Mr. Howe. "Apparently, Mr. Howe had the same question. He found three different soldiers to volunteer to put it on."

"What happened?"

"Their bodies flickered like Christmas lights

before they were thrown across the room by a burst of energy."

"Are they all right?"

"Two of them, Eli, are in a psychiatric ward."

"And the third?"

From the look my dad gives Mr. Howe, he obviously thinks it's Howe's turn to answer. But he doesn't.

"You don't have to go," Dad says softly. "You don't have to do any of this." Then, in a louder voice, he speaks to Thirty and the Twenty-Fives.

"You can't make him do any of this! And I won't. This has to stop somewhere. And it stops now! With my son."

Thirty flips on the newspaper image of Mom, stuck in 1937. I think that's a mean thing to do to my dad.

"Dr. Sands. It is our job to decide if Mr. Howe can go ahead with his operation. But our decision was made before we got here. We're in a dangerous situation. And as far as we know, your son is the best chance we have to keep it from getting worse. Eli, if something happened to Earth history back in Alexandria, to change things, to make them different for us now, you need to find a way to change it back."

"How do I know I'd go back to Alexandria?"

"There's a chance . . ." My dad lets that trail off.

"What?" I ask him.

He doesn't really want to say. "There's a *chance*, it seems, that whatever attracted you there in the first place will pull you back. You may have created a kind of particle trail connecting our time to Alexandria. Or at least connecting you."

"You think we're so heartless, Sands. Look." Mr. Howe holds up a Thickskin that looks about my size. "We've got protection for him when he gets there."

"He's not going!" It looks like Dad is about to lunge for the suit, but a couple of DARPA men block his path.

"Dad? What if I don't go?"

I look up at the wall, see Mom's face staring out from the old newspaper photograph, see it change to the pictures of the confused and scared-looking airplane passengers, then see it change again to Andrew Jackson Williams being led away by the DARPA team. Thirty can play that screen like a violin.

"What happens to the world, Dad?"

"I don't care what happens to the world anymore. I care what happens to you, Eli."

But if people are getting sick, or planes are disappearing and reappearing in the sky, or ghosts are wandering the streets, and history is spinning more and more out of control, it's not going to be much of a world for me or him, anyway. And I don't want my mom trying to survive things that happened before she was even born. I didn't ask to get all tangled up in time like this, but now, I guess, that tangling is part of me.

I reach for the hat in the metal case.

"Put on the Thickskin," Mr. Howe says.

He holds it up, and as I take a corner in my hand, Dad yells, "Eli, no!" He breaks free of the guards and runs toward the cart holding the Seals cap.

He smashes into it, fighting with the DARPA men, with Mr. Howe, even one of the Twenty-Fives. But no one notices the cap has been knocked loose and landed by my feet.

I can already feel the tingling in my toes.

For the second time in my life, I reach for it.

Then everything winks out, I cross the Fifth Dimension like a dream, and when I come to, the fire in Alexandria has already begun.

Chapter Twelve

Eli: Tunnel of the Dead

415 C.E.

It's definitely the hat.

But shooting through the Fifth Dimension like a bodysurfer, without being in a ship like Clyne's, is hard. It's like every wave pulls you under, and you feel like you're gonna upchuck when you arrive.

I'm woozy when I materialize inside the library grounds at Alexandria. No rhinos this time—just lots of statues. I'm in a tiled court-yard. It's night, and I can see the full moon through the open roof. Somewhere I hear a scratching sound.

In the distance, I can also see that a couple of the walls I'd jumped over earlier with Clyne are now on fire. I look at the blaze, look up at the giant statues that surround me, then hunch over to throw up.

Raising my head a moment later and wiping my mouth, I start to feel better.

I see the cap on the ground, and I'm about to pick it up, but this time I stop. I just got here. I'm still holding the Thickskin Mr. Howe gave me. I wrap the cap in it, touch it lightly — it seems safe to handle that way. I pick it up and put it back on my head. As long as the Thickskin holds, I'm okay.

Or at least, I would be okay if I didn't just see one of the statues start to move in the dark. . . .

No. It's not a statue. Did I say no rhinos? I was wrong. I've just puked all over the feet of one.

Even the rhino isn't sure what to make of it. I hear him snort and snuffle and paw the ground a little. Maybe he's not sure whether to be insulted or feel sorry for me.

Either way, I can't move, so it's a relief when somebody suddenly tackles me and drags me behind one of the *real* statues, where the rhino's going to have a hard time getting at me.

It's the girl. She talks to me, but I can't understand her. I've left my lingo-spot back in my own time. I like her voice, though. She sounds like she knows what she's doing, but she doesn't seem bossy about it. She just seems . . . kind of cool.

She speaks again, and I gesture that I don't understand. Then she reaches behind her ear. Clyne's given her a lingo-spot, too. She peels some of hers off, reaches over, and rubs it near the base of my skull.

"Wizard boy. You've come back." She gives me a kind of smile. Not like she thinks I'm a doofus, but like she finds me faintly amusing, anyway.

"I'm not a wizard. My name is Eli Sands. How do you do?" I hold out my hand, but she doesn't shake it. Maybe that's not the custom here. "Wow, we're really talking. I mean, I'm talking to you, but you're part of history!"

"What do you mean? Whose history?"

"Everybody's! You're living even before George Washington was born . . . or Shakespeare! You're really old!"

"You claim not to be a wizard, yet you claim to know who will be born? And for your information, rude wizard, I have lived only thirteen years."

"Look, I'm not claiming to be magic, and I didn't mean you were old like a grownup. . . ." Maybe I'm getting off on the wrong foot. I search in my pocket for something to give her as a gift. My fingers feel the baseball cards Mr. Howe had given to me. I pull one out. Ken Griffey Jr.

She looks at it, watching the holographic highlights of Griffey's career. "Perhaps you're not a wizard. I certainly don't need any cheap magic like this." She flings the card away, and it lands somewhere on the tile floor with a small *click*. "And my name is Thea, daughter of Hypatia, head librarian of Alexandria and chief lecturer in math and astronomy."

"Was that your mom with you at the lighthouse?"

"'Mom?'" Her lingo-spot translates. "You mean 'mother'?" I nod. "They took her. I watched them."

"Who?"

"Tiberius. 'Brother' Tiberius. You saw him at the lighthouse, too."

"Why does he hate you so much?"

"He thinks my mother and I are witches."

"Are you?"

She gives me the kind of mixed-up look my dad specializes in, only this one seemed to say she's mad at me, a little hurt, but still feels sorry for me, all at once.

"*Okay*, you're not a witch, and I'm not a wizard, but I *did* just come back through the Fifth Dimension. And I'm still a little foggy. And I could use your help."

"Fifth Dimension? But there are only four.

Anyway, wizard, I might need *your* help. Your lizard friend might need it, too."

"Clyne? Is he all right?"

"Yes, K'lion"—she pronounces the name in a way that makes sense to her—"is fine. I hope." She points out toward the grounds. "He is somewhere out there, trying to fix his vessel. But the zoo animals have been loose since this afternoon. The guards have fled—or gone over to Tiberius. And Tiberius himself has almost broken through the walls. Or burned his way through."

The smell of smoke is definitely getting stronger.

"He's coming here to get you?"

"Not just me. The scrolls, too. Everything. Everything the library stands for. That's why I'm taking a few things now and planning to get out."

She has a satchel over her shoulder with a few odds and ends in it. She tiptoes back toward one of the walls, and the scratching sound resumes. She's trying to chip a piece loose with a small pick she's taken out of the bag.

"What are you doing?"

"I will not let them destroy everything," she says. "This is my favorite tile and I'm taking it with me."

"What's so special about it?" I ask.

"It's a picture of my mother when she was my age. My grandfather, Theon, put it up here when he was the head librarian."

On the other side of the statues, the rhino suddenly bellows and charges, followed by a *"Tchkkk! Tchkkk! K'laaa!"* from close by.

"Who's there!" Thea yells. But we both know. There's only one voice like that on Earth.

I can't see clearly in the dark, but there's another crash, and it sounds like the rhino has stampeded right through the pillars and stumbled down the stairs.

"Poor thing. He's nearly blind, you know." Thea rises up, then shrieks as Clyne leaps down from the head of the statue above us.

"Eli Boy! *Klaak!* Hello!"

He turns to Thea. She hardly needs a lingo-spot with him—despite his *klaaaks* and *tikks,* Clyne is mostly speaking in her tongue. Their voices are too low for me to get a good translation.

Thea looks grim. "You heard him. They just broke through the walls. We need to leave."

Clyne is a bit frantic. "My ship is going to stay *gra-bakked* and never get fixed! The school's going to kill me!"

"What's '*gra-bakked*'?" I ask.

"You don't have a good word for it," he explains.

We can hear shouting in the distance but can't see anyone yet. In a few moments, Tiberius and his followers will be inside the library.

"We need to leave," Thea says slowly, "or it will not be the school that kills you."

She slashes at the wall and with a grunt, finally pulls the tile free. She tosses it in her bag and takes off in the dark. She's familiar enough with the layout of the library grounds, and Clyne, apparently, can see pretty well without light. But I keep bumping into things. I hit my right shin twice.

We get out of the courtyard, and by the time we're inside the main building we're almost running. Smoke trickles in behind us and keeps us moving along.

There's a little light now — some of the halls have torches in wall holders, and the ones that are still lit are casting long shadows. It would be fun to play with the weird shapes we're making if there was any time. But we're surrounded on both sides by stacked rows of cubbyholes — thousands of them, stretching all the way to the ceiling, holding scroll after scroll after scroll.

Thea hands me her satchel. "Hold this."

"What are you doing?" I ask.

She doesn't answer me directly but keeps moving down the halls, plucking scrolls out of the shelves almost randomly. She glances at them and shouts out the subject matter, almost angrily, as she gives them to me to stuff into the bag.

"Planetary motion!" she shouts. "Healing with plants! . . . *A History of Atlantis*! . . . Maps of the world!"

She keeps going, taking what she can, practically tossing them to me, as the bag gets heavier and heavier.

"Jewish history! . . . Roman history! . . . Egyptian history! . . . Secret history!" More scrolls.

"*The Frogs* and *The Birds*," she yells.

"Do you study nature?" I ask, panting a little as I try to keep up with her.

"Those are the names of plays!"

Clyne has taken a cue from her and jumped up to the top of the shelves, running above us, grabbing scrolls from the top shelves and flinging them down, even carrying one in his mouth like a pirate holding a knife.

I guess he thinks he's helping, but there's hardly any room left in the bag.

"This is getting pretty heavy," I tell Thea.

She turns to face me with more scrolls in her arms. *"The Proper Care of Chimaeras and Other Rare Beasts,"* she says, sticking another one into the satchel, "and *How to Build a Pyramid.*"

She stands, looking right into my eyes. "I have to save what little I can."

What can I tell her? I'm about to offer to put one in my back pocket, but then we hear voices. Not ours. They're coming from behind us.

"But I suppose I have to save all of us, too. Come on." She's running again, but this time there aren't any more stops to save scrolls.

"Where are we going?" I ask.

"Underneath."

Clyne jumps down and follows behind us.

A few more twists and turns, and the walls of cubbyholes open up into what looks like a kind of ancient apartment, or maybe a fancy Las Vegas hotel room: a couple of low beds, a table with parchment and more scrolls piled on it, bowls of fruit set out everywhere, a couple of chin-high statues, and piles of clothes draped over the carved marble chairs. Large pillows and cushions are scattered everywhere.

"What's this?"

"Our living quarters," Thea tells me. "There's an entrance here that goes down to the cata-combs."

"What's a catacomb?"

"Tunnels under the city. We can head away from here, out past the necropolis, past the city gates, and try to get away."

"What's a necropolis?"

She stares at me a moment. "Do you not go to gymnasium?"

"I get my exercise."

"Gymnasium! A *school*!" She throws up her hands. "Necropolis is a city of the dead! The tunnel out of Alexandria goes through it."

"Yum!"

That was Clyne. Both Thea and I turn to see him eating an orange from one of the bowls. "Orrranngge! *Brkkk!* No thing like it at home! Snacked one previous from an outside tree!"

Thea shakes her head. "He has been eating them all afternoon. He's never seen them before. Tell me, what world do the two of you come from? I realize this isn't the only planet in the universe."

Clyne answers her. "Not just! *Cmmk!* This isn't the only universe in the universe, either!"

"Mother always said the same thing. I should write that down. But there isn't time." Thea goes over to the marble desk and tries to move it with her shoulder. It doesn't budge. She knocks a couple of half-finished scrolls off the top and picks one up to look at it. "This is Mother's work. This one is about slow pox." She throws it down. "It doesn't matter now, does it?"

I pick it up and stuff it in the satchel. If it can help Mr. Howe, it can help get my mom back. "It matters to some of us, Thea."

"At the moment, moving this desk matters even more. The entrance to the tunnel is underneath."

Clyne and I help her push. As we huff and

puff, I ask her about slow pox. I don't want to seem too eager.

"You don't want to know. Uhhh . . ." The desk is starting to budge. "It saps the life out of you—and the spirit. And leaves a wrinkled shell of a body afterward. According to my mother, it jumped from goats and sheep to people. No one believes her."

But I might. Or someone else in the future.

We've moved the desk a couple feet; there's a large hole in the floor, like a sewer opening with the cover taken away. Which, in a way, I guess it is.

"If we go through the necropolis, there'll be fresh bodies in there. From the pox. If it's any comfort, by the time someone's dead, they can't spread the contagion. Still, we will have to make our way past them very carefully in the dark."

I don't say okay to that, but I don't say no either. The air is getting smokier, and I know we have to get out. We push the desk another foot over when we hear them:

"DEMON!"

I think they mean Clyne. There are two of them, from Tiberius's group, standing at the entrance to the room. One holds a sword. One is enough.

"Come on!" Thea grabs my arm and pulls me down into the hole. We roll down a muddy slope into pitch blackness. I stand up, relieved not to bump my head. We're definitely in a tunnel, and I can't see a thing.

"We need a torch," Thea says. We're also missing a dinosaur. I hear more shouting from above, followed by a *brkkk!* and an *akkk!* or two.

"What about Clyne?"

"The lizard god's on his own right now."

"But I can't just—"

"They already took my mother. Who knows what they did to her. But they will do it to us. And we won't be able to help anyone. Come on!"

Then more commotion at the tunnel entrance, and with a loud screeching sound,

Clyne catapults himself down in the darkness. We hear him tumble, then in the next moment he jumps past us. "Go! Angry mammals above!"

Someone who *does* have a torch pops his head down under the floor and peers after us. I think I can make out a scraggly kind of beard in the shadows. "They're down here!"

Tiberius has joined the party.

Thea and I break into another run. I feel around in my pockets for a match, anything, but all I touch are the other two baseball cards. I take one out. . . . The faint, dim glow from the holographic image—in the dark, I can just make out Barry Bonds—lights up a square inch in front of my face. Better than nothing.

It smells pretty damp and sour, but I don't care. I just hope I have enough light to keep us from crashing into a pillar or running off the embankment into the slow, gurgling stream below.

"Just follow the water!" Thea pants.

"How . . . how are you going so fast . . . ?" I can hardly see her ahead of me in the dark.

"I'm holding on to K'lion's tail!"

We open a lead on Tiberius, because his men seem a little scared to come after us in the dark. In case Thea really is a witch. Or I'm a wizard. Or Clyne is whatever they think he is.

All those thoughts are knocked out of my head when the three of us go crashing down as we all trip over loose . . .

. . . *bodies* that have been dragged into the catacombs and left there.

I crash down right next to one as Barry Bonds pops out of my hand and falls next to Thea, who's landed near me. As my eyes adjust, I can still barely make her out. "Slow pox," she whispers. "They don't even have time to bury them anymore."

I can see her reaching out in the dark and, like a blind person, touching the faces of the bodies that have been dumped there, trying to figure out what they look like with her fingers.

Maybe in case one of them is her mother.

I sit there for a second, trying to watch her in the dark.

What do you say to someone in that situation?

I won't find out. Torches flicker in the distance—some of the mob has gotten over whatever spooked them, and they're back on our heels.

And where is . . . "Clyne? Buddy? Are you out there?"

"No talk." It turns out dinosaurs can *whisper.* "This is a move in Cacklaw. Play dead. Fake out." I can't see him, but he must be lying perfectly still, pretending to be a dead human body so that Tiberius won't notice him in the dark.

I'm not sure that will work. For one thing, water has begun to steadily drip down on us, and it's hard not to move.

"Get away from here, Clyne! Run. We'll come after you." I hiss-whisper back, and hope the sound doesn't carry too far in the tunnel.

"Can't go, *kk-kk-kk,*" Clyne answers. "You

and Thea still here. I hide, too." I hear a loud *splash* as Clyne dives into the stream.

"Up ahead!" The torches are getting closer.

Thea is still carefully touching the faces of the bodies around her.

"Don't move," I hiss again.

From the footsteps, I can tell they're nearly on us. I shut up and roll over, lying still, but I bump the decaying body next to me, and part of it gives way with a *squish*, like a Jell-O mold collapsing. The whole thing is really gross, but there isn't much time to be scared. The men are too close.

"We'll never find them down here, Tiberius."

"We will. Heaven commands us to."

"This place, Tiberius, has little to do with heaven."

"You are a nervous fool, Praetorius."

"Only a fool would *not* be nervous. It is dark. Our clothes are heavy with water, and these pillars are groaning. And I can smell smoke even down here. You should not have let this grow out of control."

"The fire started at the harbor. There was a ship . . . bringing in more scrolls for that witch-woman's library. Foreign scrolls. The crowd wanted to put a stop . . . to strange ideas. The flames are a sign of their righteous passion."

"All this death down here . . . it's evil."

"Listen. Shh."

"What?"

"Hear that? Like a faint echo."

I peek and see Tiberius peering in our direction. The water is coming in more heavily. Some gets on my face, and I try not to sputter.

"Death is natural, Praetorius. But life, spinning out of control—*that* is evil." There's a constant rumble now as water comes in. But that's not our only problem: Tiberius is staring right where Thea has wedged herself between a couple of bodies.

"Tiberius? What do you see?"

"I believe I see a strange twist of fate, Praetorius—or a witch's trick."

He steps toward Thea just as the rumble turns into a low, steady roar, and then it feels like I'm back in the Fifth Dimension, because several things happen at once:

Tiberius touches Thea, who stops pretending to be dead long enough to scream.

Tiberius screams back, "Sorceress! I *have* you!"

As he grabs for her, I reach out and yank his ankle. I guess he thinks Thea is bringing the dead to life, because his scream changes from rage to terror . . .

. . . just as water sprays down on his torch, snuffing it out and surrounding all of us with total darkness . . .

. . . just as whatever was controlling the flow of water into the harbor gives way, and half the Mediterranean comes roaring into the catacombs and sweeps us up. I reach out for Thea, for someone or something to hold on to, but grab only water, which fills my ears, my eyes, my nose . . .

. . . and then I go black. And this time, there are no colors to wake up to.

Chapter Thirteen

Thea: Survivor's Tale

415 C.E.

After seeing so much, it would have been far easier to tell myself I had gone mad. I was soaking wet and trapped in the lighthouse, where a mob had assembled—for the second time that day—calling for me to be burned. Mother was gone, taken by the same crowd, and I was left with a talking reptile and a boy trying to be a wizard as friends. And my city was burning. How much easier to tell myself it was all some kind of insane vision. But the vision wasn't insane. The city and its people were.

I had been with my mother, Hypatia, in that very lighthouse the day before as she conducted an experiment on the nature of time. That had been at noon.

By then, Mother already stood accused of being a witch. Me too, not only for being her daughter, but also for knowing stars the way I do and for suggesting once that our Earth is not the center of divine creation, but a piece of it.

Just for surviving the flood in the catacombs, they would suspect me of black magic. Eli the boy wizard, K'lion the lizard man, and I were all in the tunnels, trying to escape from the great library, which had been put to flame.

I am glad, at least, that Mother did not see the fire. It would have broken her heart and her spirit at last.

"Sorceress!" they were yelling from outside.

Me, sorceress. Here I was, a thirteen-year-old girl, shivering and cold. Where was my magic now?

In the catacombs, the docks and channel

locks had collapsed above us, destroyed by flames.

I was covered with water and swept away. I had been pretending to be dead and now found myself clutching one of the many *real* dead bodies rushing by, using it as a raft. That body, that person whose life had been given to slow pox, saved mine in the flood. Eventually, I floated out past the shattered Gate of the Moon at city's edge. I shook myself off and staggered to shore.

I gazed back where the docks had been. Fire seemed to be everywhere.

I remember once looking at a statue of Serapis—the serpent god, the healer, the city's protector—on Mother's desk. I asked her if there really was a Serapis. I argued with her that if a god, or gods, exist, how could their greatness and mystery be contained in a mere statue?

"What there is really," she said, "what exists, is people's hope that there's a way to balance things, heal them and make them better. 'Serapis' is one of the names we put to that hope."

"Then Serapis is not real?"

"Hope is a very real, very living thing. But it needs to be taken care of and nourished, or it dies."

Brother Tiberius's view was that if you even *mention* Serapis, you should have your tongue cut out.

That seemed neither helpful nor hopeful.

And now our city was burning. There were screams in the distance, panic. Everyone going through their own sorrow, their own grief.

Walking along the ruined shoreline, I heard the flapping of wings. I expected an owl hunting in the night, but saw instead the escaped griffin vulture from the zoo circling overhead. These loose bodies would be a feast for him.

Eventually, heading in the direction of the lighthouse, I was surprised to see the long wooden footbridge leading out to Pharos Island still intact. Once again, that bridge provided the promise of escape.

I thought that perhaps nobody would think to look for me in the lighthouse a second time, but I had only just arrived inside and bolted the door when I heard a loud *thump* and the first cry of "Witch!"

Tiberius had eyes all over the city, and the fire had not managed to blind them to my whereabouts. It seemed his whole mob was after a final reckoning with their perceived enemies that night.

An hour or two went by, and from the yelling, I could tell the crowd below had grown in size.

I had no idea if my new friends were still alive. Or if Mother was. In a lighthouse, surrounded by people, I had never felt more alone.

I thought of letting the mob in. Perhaps, in the end, that would be less painful.

Then, suddenly, came a new and distinct pounding on the door below. I froze, listening to the loud booms. And realized they had a battering ram. Now it didn't matter what I did. They would get in anyway.

The battering ram crashed into the door again, and instinctively, at the top of the tower, I stepped back away from the noise. I stumbled over the remains from Mother's experiment.

Because of the chaos in Alexandria, no one had come here to spark the lighthouse bonfire, which is why the signal was dark for the first time in memory. But the mirrors were there, and the fuel lines from the ground floor were still intact, drawing up oil from below to keep the giant wick lit. . . .

I realized *I* could make the lighthouse shine again if there were a way to start the fire. And perhaps, seeing the signal, someone would come. Someone not connected to the mob below.

The crystals were sharp in my hands, almost cutting my skin, but I hardly noticed. I began to wonder if those two stones could be used . . . like flints.

Chapter Fourteen

Eli: Tiberius

415 C.E.

My mom is waking me up, and I'm home in New Jersey, and it's all been a dream, and I'm still a regular kid who thinks clocks and time only move forward. It's sunny out, and I'm getting ready to go out to the woods and set up a Barnstormer game with Andy. Later, we'll get a ride home, with some warm cookies—

"Wake up, boy!"

No we won't.

I'm actually cold and soaked, and the light and warmth I feel come from the fire burning through the city of Alexandria. And instead of

my mother, I get the face of Tiberius, caked
with blood and grime and smoke. The scariest
thing of all is that he's *smiling* at me, like he's
happy that I'm still alive. Grownups always
smile at weird times—but this grin is the
weirdest and most frightening of them all.

"Wake *up*! It's not your dying time yet, wizard." He pulls me to my feet. I'm still bleary, but
I can see another body on the ground nearby.
One of his friends from the catacombs. Tiberius
points a bony finger down at his remains.

"My friend Praetorius drowned in the flood,
but *you*, warlock, you live with the help of
your dark magic."

I *am* alive, I guess. Barely. I have no idea
what happened to Thea or Clyne, though. I
mumble something to Tiberius.

"What?"

I mumble it again—I want to point out that
he's alive, too—but he still doesn't understand. I feel behind my ear—the lingo-spot
is still stuck to me. But, of course, Tiberius

doesn't have one, so he has no idea what I'm saying.

"Are you trying to cast spells on me, warlock!? Your words will not touch me, because I am protected by God's love," he screams. "His *love!*"

I repeat the word *love,* almost like a question, because it seems so out of place, but I have water in my mouth and I'm numb, so it seems like I'm spitting, and Tiberius shakes me some more.

"You think you can mock me because Alexandria is still the devil's place! But the fire of justice will cleanse it! And come morning, you will be in no position to mock me."

I hurt all over as I'm yanked around, thinking, *This would be a really good moment to get unstuck in time and be somewhere else.*

If I can just get the Thickskin off my cap and let it come in direct contact with me. . . .

But there's nothing on my head. My WOMPER-charged Seals cap is gone!

The last thing I remember is frantically trying to swim in the great gush of water and getting slammed against a pillar. The water roared by, taking me with it, and I landed—ouch!—hard on the ground, just like now, as Tiberius throws me down. I realize I'm missing a shoe, too, then pat myself down. Amazingly, I still have the last of Mr. Howe's baseball cards stuck in my pocket, and the satchel is still wrapped around me, though it's tangled up like seaweed.

Oh, no. The scrolls are gone. Except for one, stuck in the bottom of the bag.

I sit up on the ground, shivering, and it occurs to me that all I have left in the world—in *this* world—are my pants (which are torn, by the way), my shirt, and one shoe. And worst of all, no cap. Does this mean I'm stuck here?

Tiberius looks like maybe he's ready to throw me back down again. "Suddenly, you're no longer so powerful, are you, warlock?"

"Tiberius!"

He must have followers all over the city. Three men run down the main boulevard toward the shore, making their way to him, jumping over rubble on the ground. Two of them hold torches, and the third one, a spear.

As they step over the smoking ruins next to us, I realize that whatever building or structure was here, it was probably standing yesterday when I flew over it with Clyne. Was that really less than a day ago?

Tiberius's followers make a big fuss over him, checking to see if he's all right. They're whispering, so the lingo-spot isn't picking it all up, but they're pointing to me, and I hear stray phrases like "boy-witch," and "not much longer," neither of which makes me happy. After they get done talking about me, they start pointing at the lighthouse.

But the lighthouse is dark, so I wonder what they think they see.

Then I hear what sounds like "Thea" coming from one of them, and Tiberius gets even more excited.

Spear-man gives me a small, quick jab in the shoulder to get me moving.

I wonder if this is what war is like—being this scared, and not knowing if you're going to make it. I limp along, hopping a lot on my one shoe, trying to avoid all the sharp pieces of wood and hot ashes with the other, bare foot.

We're heading back toward the lighthouse.

And then we stop: Suddenly, brilliantly, the lighthouse flame roars to life! So brightly, none of us can even look directly at the beam. Someone's in there. . . .

Thea!

I hope.

Alive! And so's the tower. And so are Tiberius and his henchmen, who're now running to get there. I do a full-speed hop to try and get there ahead of them.

But that makes Spear-man unhappy. He catches up with me and shoves me hard with the blunt end of his weapon again, making me stumble forward, right on my bare foot.

He makes it clear that next time it won't be the blunt end. As I pick myself up, my hand comes across the surviving baseball card in my shirt and I hear Tiberius hissing something about "the witch" again, and I get an idea.

By the time we get to the rickety footbridge leading to the island, more people have fallen in with us. Some are followers of Tiberius; others just seem to be scared, townsfolk drawn to the one beam of light that's not going to hurt them.

I'm pretty sure I could slip away in the crowd pouring off the bridge before Spear-man could come after me, but then I think of how Clyne stayed with us in the tunnel when he didn't have to. I guess that's what makes all this different from Barnstormers, or any of the Comnet games: There's no reloading or starting over. Instead, there's just living with every decision you make.

BOOM!

Some of Tiberius's gang are already here,

pounding on the door with a makeshift battering ram, a piece of wood they've salvaged from
the burning city.

The door to the lighthouse is already starting to splinter. If it is Thea who's in there,
she's in trouble.

Tiberius, Spear-man, and everybody else
wait for the door to crack so they can charge
inside. Even though none of us can look
directly at the light overhead, enough of it
spills over our faces that I can see everybody is
excited in a strange way. Like the look I'd see
on Mr. Howe's face, sometimes, when he'd
talk about Dad's work being used to make
new weapons.

My hands slip around my baseball card
again—it's the McGwire 'gram—and while
everybody's distracted, I make my move.

I scream and run in front of the battering
ram, putting myself between it and the door.

Everyone stops for a moment, because my
action is so unexpected. "People!" I shout.
"Behold!" I'm not sure any of them understand

exactly what I'm saying, but that sounds like wizard talk to me, and they all look when I pull out the McGwire card and hold it up. What they're seeing is the 'gram playing McGwire's Hall-of-Fame induction speech, but that's not what I tell them.

"Genie!" I scream. "Genie!"

I hear the word *djinn* repeated back slowly by one or two of them, so I know some of them get it, and they look at each other, and then back at me. "Wizard!" I yell, pointing at myself. Then I wave the McGwire card around some more, letting them think there's a little shrunken man captured inside. I hope they'll accept the idea that not every genie has to live in a lamp.

I point to myself again—"Wizard!"—then the card—"Genie!"—then put my hand on the lighthouse door. "No."

I hope I've made my case and scared them off. I don't have any backup plan.

At a minimum, I've succeeded in confusing everyone. They've all stopped what they were doing. I think some of them understand what I'm threatening. Or pretending to threaten.

I keep standing in front of the lighthouse. My foot hurts.

Tiberius walks up. "Boy. Your magic won't work here. Your tricks are no good." But he doesn't seem a hundred percent sure of that and keeps a little distance between us. I shake the McGwire card at him, like a rattle. He takes a step back.

It's a standoff for about thirty seconds. Then he decides to call my bluff. "If you have any other magic left, you'd better use it now." He turns to face the crowd. "Seize the wizard and hold him! We'll burn him with the witch! We'll burn them in this tower!"

A lot of the townspeople aren't sure. But Spear-man and some of the battering-ram guys are. They move toward me.

"Wizard, wizard, wizard!" I shout, scooting away from them. "I'm a wizard!"

But Tiberius's henchmen are still coming at

me. In another second or two they'll have me cornered. "I am . . . a . . . wizard!" I yell again.

But they've all stopped looking at me, and I realize the lighthouse door is open. Thea is standing there.

"Wazir," she says.

Everyone's amazed to see her. She walks right up to me, right in front of Tiberius. "We pronounce the word 'wazir' here."

"You're alive," I say.

"So far," she replies. Then she turns to the crowd. "The lighthouse on Pharos burns again. But it is up to all of you"—and she points to the whole tattered, smoky, confused, angry crowd—"to decide what kind of light falls on Alexandria. *His*"—and here she points to Tiberius—"or your own."

That's it. That's where she leaves it. Now the crowd is totally confused—they actually have to make a choice.

"Man," I whisper to her. "You're really brave."

"I am terrified," she says, "but I heard you down here. You too are brave, boy wizard. I decided to stand with you."

For a moment, it seems like Thea's tactic is working even better than my wizard trick with the baseball card.

But only for a moment. "How long," Tiberius says in a loud voice, "will we let witches lie to us?" He allows the question to sink in for effect. "Get them both!"

"Genie, genie, genie!" I scream, hoping that might scare enough of them, but nobody seems to be buying it now. Spear-man has his weapon raised, and I don't know if he's going to get me or Thea first. I'm scared, too, crying really, wondering how grownups ever got to be so messed up to begin with. I squeeze my eyes shut. "Genie . . . ," I whisper, clutching the card.

"Aakkkk! Ouch! Wet! Hello!"

It's Clyne, coming out of the sea, bounding toward the lighthouse. You'd almost swear there was a smile on his long gray face.

Tons of people scream and run away.

"Bad night," Clyne says. "Strange mammals."

"Dragon!" Tiberius spits, but he's definitely backing away, too.

"Big flood," Clyne says to us. "*Gkkkk. . . .* Uncertain if you mammals thrive in water or not. Glad you're dry now."

"I'm not exactly dry," I say, "but I'm all right. What about you?"

"Been swimming awhile. Found this." He holds up the waterlogged Seals cap. "Know it emits . . . *tk-tk-tk* . . . a small time disturbance. Time goofs can be traced!" He pulls what looks like a small Geiger counter out of his jumpsuit. It makes loud clicks and everyone left in the crowd who didn't flee at "Dragon!" jumps back.

"Full of sad thoughts when I found your head garment but not your head. Then my eyes glanced Thea's mighty blaze. Here." He tosses the cap at me. *"Kk-kang!* Can't travel time without a swift key to Dimension Five."

I put the cap on and cold seawater runs

down my face. Most of the protective Thick-skin is gone, and I can already feel the familiar tingling.

"No!" Tiberius shouts, as I begin fading away. He reaches and grabs Thea, who scratches long red welts across his face, and I have just enough time to grab her back.

We're holding on to each other, and now it's my turn to act like a time-ship. When I get jerked across the Fifth Dimension, Thea comes with me.

It's only Clyne who gets left behind.

Chapter Fifteen

Eli: Many Happy Returns
August 23, 2019 C.E.

Thea and I return, materializing just outside Moonglow at night. We fade in next to a series of new generators that have been installed behind the building. They've really built the place up since I've been gone, but how long has that been?

I'm feeling a little wobbly, as usual, but Thea is worse — shivering, her teeth chattering, trying to pull the remains of her robes around her. We're both still soaked — more than sixteen hundred years after getting wet.

"Where . . . ? Where . . . ?" she manages to ask.

"Home," I say. Meaning, my home, or what's been passing for home ever since Mom vanished and Dad and I left Princeton.

I'm still tingling. I need to get the cap off my head before it sends me back through the time stream, but I don't want to touch it myself. Hurrying, I take Thea's hand and use it to yank the Seals cap off my head.

"What are you doing?" she asks, pulling her arm back.

"I'm sorry. The cap and me, we're two parts of a whole. It creates a reaction . . . that causes my time traveling. If I want to stay put, I can't wear it."

"I am traveling with a wizard," she sighs, "who has an enchanted hat he cannot control."

Since I don't have any Thickskin left, I take a stick, lift up the cap, and hide it in the hollow of an oak a few yards away.

I turn back and squint into the bright lights surrounding the winery. Realizing how exposed we are, I tap Thea on the shoulder to get her to go a little deeper into the grove of trees with me, until we figure out what to do.

But she's mesmerized by the electric lights. Of course. She's never seen them before.

I hear heavy boot steps. "Come on!" I tell her. But she doesn't want to move. "Come *on!*" Reluctantly, she goes with me. Huddling behind a tree, I see a couple soldiers walk by in uniforms I don't recognize from DARPA. The situation at Moonglow must have grown bigger and more serious, and I figure it'd be better if Thea didn't come to Mr. Howe's attention at all.

"Listen." I try to whisper, but it comes out faster and louder than I want. "I have a hideout here in the woods."

"Where?" she asks again, and it occurs to me that so much has happened to Thea, she might still think she's back in Alexandria somewhere, having a really strange dream. One with electric lights in it.

"This way," I tell her. We race past more oaks in the dark, stumbling a little, though her footing is at least as steady as mine. She must be feeling a little bit better, or she's a really great sleepwalker.

When we reach Wolf House, I show her how to climb through the holes in the fence, and we step carefully around the stone ruins. I take Thea down to where the basement was supposed to be—a big, boxy area that was used for storing coal. Now it's more like a fort, where you can look out and see anybody who's coming before they see you.

But the old stone walls don't warm her at all, and she still shivers. "We need to build a fire," she says.

"I don't have a lighter or matches," I tell her.

"You mean, something to spark the flame?" She looks around, then gathers some sticks and rocks in her hands. "Let me."

Thea wipes her face and for the first time really takes in her surroundings—the trees, the crumbling house. "Your world isn't so different from mine," she says. "Not quite as built up, maybe."

She hasn't seen a traffic jam yet, or a crowd at a ballgame, or the skyscrapers in a million different places, like San Francisco or New York. The world seems pretty built up to *me*. I hope I get a chance to show her those things someday.

Right now, we have more pressing needs. Like getting warm. And getting help. I have to figure out a way to get my dad here to explain what's going on. "Thea, I have to go back there to the lab."

"You're leaving me?" She looks a little confused, like maybe she's lapsed back into that dream state. "What is a 'lab'?"

"I have to get help. From my father. And a lab is a place where we do experiments. Science."

"Like a gymnasium?"

"Like a gymnasium. You should be okay here for a little while. Hide if you need to. I won't be long."

She gives me a look that says *I hope not*. I can tell even in the dark.

I head toward the winery. Somehow the path back is harder without Thea. I trip over a couple fallen branches I didn't see before, but I get there. And when I do, this time I walk right in the front door.

"My God. You came back." It's Mr. Howe, who emerges almost immediately. His comment makes me wonder if he really expected me to come back at all, in which case, why was he so slaphappy about sending me off into time in the first place?

Two guys in particularly thick Thickskins emerge and scan me up and down. Some kind of bug alarm, I think. Right. I could be carrying slow pox or something else. A third guy comes out of the lab and takes off his hood. I recognize him from the BART tunnel: one of the Twenty-Fives.

"I want to see my dad."

Howe exchanges glances with Twenty-Five. "We haven't seen him, Eli. He's been gone for a couple of days. We were about to ask you."

I groan. "Don't tell me he got sucked into the time stream, too?"

"He just drove away in his truck the other day. *Ran* away. He was getting depressed that you hadn't come back."

"How long have I been gone?"

"Three weeks, now."

"But I was only gone for a night."

Mr. Howe makes a note of that.

Having scanned every tangled inch of me, the Thickskin guys appear to be steering me to Dad's lab. I stop suddenly. They bump into each other, like a pair of bowling pins. "Why are we going in there if my dad's gone? Who's running his lab?"

"We have to do more tests, Eli. Find out what's happened to you." Then Howe lowers his voice, as if he's telling me a secret. "Find out more about the effects of time displacement on human beings."

"I'm soaking wet."

"From time displacement?" He makes another note.

"From water. Do you think I could get something to eat? And change my clothes first?"

More notes. I'm also still feeling a little queasy, which *is* from the time travel, but I'm not gonna tell him that, 'cause that'll mean an extra hour or two of tests.

"We'd rather you didn't."

"I'm about to faint."

Howe looks at Twenty-Five, who nods. "You can change your clothes, but you can't eat yet. Put your clothes in here." He hands me a plastic bag. "We want to test them for WOMPER radiation."

Mr. Howe orders a soldier to go with me. "Make sure he stays put! But first . . ."

Howe carefully pulls some Thickskin over his hands and takes the satchel from around my neck. It's soaked, too, and tangled with my jacket. I had hardly noticed it was still there. But Howe caught a glimpse of the lone surviving scroll from the library peeking out of the bag. And now he holds it — very carefully — in his hand.

"Perfect," he says, looking at it.

"I don't know what it's about," I tell him. "It could be slow pox. It could be Atlantis. It could be a million things."

"It hardly even matters," Howe tells me. Before I can ask him why, he's talking to the soldier again. "Definitely make sure he stays put."

I'm trying to figure out a way to lose this guy, but he's sticking right next to me.

Heading toward my room, we pass one of Moonglow's limestone caves full of old wine barrels. Getting an idea, I take off and sprint inside. "Hey!" the guard yells after me.

I have just enough of a head start to duck behind some of the barrels. But he's only a few feet behind, and he'll find me right away . . . unless . . .

"Come on, kid, come out of there. What's the use? You can't hide in here very long."

I touch the lingo-spot behind my ear. I slowly peel it off my skin. I hate to give it up so easily . . .

. . . but without thinking about it too much longer, I stick it onto one of the barrels near the guard. "Hey!" he says. "Come on!"

Now, peeled off me, the lingo-spot doesn't stay calibrated for English and goes back to default mode: dinosaur talk. *"Brrrrk! Braaak!"* The guard jumps. Every time he speaks, his translated voice comes out sounding kind of like Clyne's.

He hears it, and he's not sure who's talking. "Who's there? Kid?"

"Tkkk ka kaa kaaaa."

"Who is that?" he says, getting a little more freaked out.

Again, he hears his own question repeated in Saurian. He unhooks his gun from his holster. When he gets close enough to start peering into barrels, I tiptoe out behind him, then tear off down the hall.

By the time anyone spots me, I'm through the old kitchen in the lunchroom and out through one of the side windows.

•   •   •

I'm in a full run to Wolf House, and I'm winded when I finally see the fire that Thea has going. But I gasp when I see she has company: Clyne. And my father.

I'm not sure which one of them amazes me more. Clyne's time-vessel, with its still-fresh rhino dents, is parked where horse-drawn wagons were once supposed to come to Wolf House's front doors. He fixed his ship somehow, which explains, kind of, how he got here. But what about Sandusky?

"Dad?"

After all that's happened, he doesn't know what to say to me at first. I can't really blame him. So he doesn't say anything. He hugs me.

"Dad. They said you'd disappeared, too. I thought maybe . . . you'd gone after Mom."

"I had to get away from the lab. I had to get away from *them*. I've been hiding out. But I'd check by here a couple of times a day. I figured this is where you'd go if you came back. *When* you came back." He seems relieved that it turned out to be "when," after all.

"I've met your friends," he adds.

"*Aaak!* Nice sire man! Met *k-kk-kkk* your father." Clyne seems happy to see me. It's almost like he'd give me a hug, too . . . except there's a big gash on his left arm. It doesn't seem to faze him. "Being raised by a single parent of each gender is unique and worth studying!"

Thea is pressing a damp bunch of leaves against Clyne's wound. "Thea . . . ," I say to her, and realize that while she can understand me, I'm once again without a lingo-spot. She gives me a little smile, but she's crying, too.

"Clyne here's been translating," Dad says. Then he pulls me aside and whispers, "Is he from another planet, or another time?"

I whisper back, "Both. He's a dinosaur. Evolved. Like us."

I turn to Clyne. "How'd you get out?"

"Not easy, with so many mad mammals tail-close. Good leg jumps help—*pa pa pa paaak!*—landing me dab-smack in the light tower!" He pats his time-ship. "Found Thea leftovers —"

Thea hears her name and says something to Clyne. Whatever it is causes him to nod in a gentle way. "Her mother's *kris-talls*," he continues, trying out the word, "very helpful in reconstructing engine — *gra-bakk*ness in time-vessel."

"What's '*gra-bakk*'?" my dad asks.

"We don't really have a word for it," I explain.

"But chrono-compass is half-right now," Clyne continues.

"Half?" I ask.

"Can't *fft-tt-kkk!* blaze new time paths now. Can retrace old ones. Tracks particle residue of time travelers . . . *skkk*. Found my way back following you and Thea. Do a d-jump home, next stop, maybe in time for class."

"What's a 'd-jump'?" Dad asks.

"We probably don't have a word for it," I tell him.

"Dimension jump," Clyne explains. Then he shakes his head in a very human way. "Teachers will unbelieve stories of this Earth. Dancing mammals! Failing marks for me. *K-tng!* Even with proof."

"Proof?"

"Look."

I go over to peer inside the ship, and the light from the fire is just enough to let me see the pile of scrolls Clyne must have pulled out from the library flames after we left. Most of them are scorched.

"Many mammal fires," Clyne says. "Had to get going, or more would be brought."

I look back to see if this cheers Thea up, but it doesn't.

"What's wrong?"

My dad looks sad. "Apparently, Clyne told her what happened to her mother."

"What?"

"She didn't make it."

I turn to Thea. "I'm sorry."

That makes Dad bring up the question of *my*

mother. "I've been studying some recent history, myself. Took one of your Comnet screens so that I could read up on the 1930s and '40s. Trying to find out what happened to Margarite."

"And?"

"Don't know. Yet. Haven't found anything. That *Chronicle* article is the last report we have."

Thea is still dressing Clyne's wound, but there isn't time for it. "They'll be here fast," I tell them. "They'll be after me." I look at Clyne and Thea. "The two of you need to get going. If they catch you, they'll turn you into lab specimens. You'll never be free."

"It's true," Dad agrees. "Look what happened to us."

Clyne looks over to Thea, and without saying anything, invites her onto his ship.

With the campfire behind her, Thea looks kind of smart and heroic, even though she's wiping her eyes. She looks . . . *cool.* And I don't just mean for a girl.

"It's a long goodbye," Clyne agrees. "But I'll probably return with my teacher *k-k-kkkatt!* to show what I've been through and fix back my scores." He extends his hand to Thea. "You can come to class. Together, we'll win every science fair."

Thea's about to step into the ship when she stops and does something totally embarrassing.

She thanks me.

I could tell that's what she was doing. I didn't have to know the exact words she was saying. But that wasn't the embarrassing part. It was the kiss on the cheek.

"Yeah, yeah, sure. No problem," I say quickly.

"Yes, gratitude!" Clyne says, and as cheerful as he tries to be, he can't help wincing as he moves his wounded arm.

He's about to follow Thea into the ship when the light from the campfire explodes. At least, that's how it seems when a row of spotlights get flipped on, each one held by a

DARPA soldier. The new light reveals other DARPA henchmen carrying guns. Mr. Howe is with them, along with the lone Twenty-Five. "Nobody should be leaving just yet," Mr. Howe says.

"This is a severe security breach, Eli," he continues. "You've brought living organisms with you back through the time stream."

Clyne takes another step toward his ship.

"Don't do that," Mr. Howe tells him.

Clyne shakes his head. "All the time, angry mammals! Like big Saurian carnivores with empty stomachs!"

All the soldiers step back when Clyne speaks. "You talk," Mr. Howe says to him.

"You, too!" Clyne chirps agreeably.

"I can't let you leave."

"We can't let you stay," Dad mutters under his breath.

"Sorry. Bye!" Clyne steps toward the ship, and all the DARPA men raise their guns.

My hands fumble nervously in my pocket. I

still have the Mark McGwire card that I used in Alexandria.

But right here, right now, I'm not a wizard. The card won't spook anybody. But then I realize that sometimes the most amazing trick of all, the one that can be hardest to do, is simply standing up for what you know is right.

"I'm your secret weapon!" I yell back at Mr. Howe, jumping between Clyne and the guns. "I'm your Danger Boy! You can't let them hurt me."

There's a long pause as everyone considers what I just said.

"Right?" I add hopefully.

"We wouldn't hurt anybody," Mr. Howe says, almost whining. "The ammo in these guns is just for *tranquilizing*. So step away from there."

Nobody does.

Clyne moves, and I adjust my position to stay between him and the guns.

"Gratitude! *Kkkh!*" Clyne whispers to me. "When I move, you fall."

I'm not sure what he's talking about.

"I can't let you get back to that ship," Mr. Howe says. Apparently, that's not what Clyne has in mind. He performs a jump that—if this was a basketball championship—would lead the highlight reels for all time. He leaps up high enough to kick shut the door to his ship, locking Thea inside. Off the door, he catapults himself backward through the air. Before the guns start firing, I hit the ground.

"Eli!" my father screams.

Clyne's ship starts taking off—either with Thea guiding it or the ship guiding itself. Twenty-Five pulls a weapon out of his jacket, which is definitely *not* a tranquilizer gun. He aims it at the vessel, and a long beam comes out, glances off the ship, and causes it to wobble.

But the ship vanishes anyway. The other men are aiming at Clyne, who keeps jumping and somersaulting farther away. Twenty-Five lowers his gun, and I rise up to put myself between him and Clyne again.

I buy just enough time so Clyne can disappear into the trees. Twenty-Five keeps the gun raised in my direction, but Mr. Howe forces his hand down while waving the DARPA men into the woods to try and capture Clyne on foot.

So I'm not a genie, but at least I helped my friend.

My dad, however, doesn't fare so well.

One of the tranquilizer darts—I hope that's what they really are—is sticking out of him. Right near his hip. He looks at me; his eyes widen a little, then he crumples over.

I race over to him and hold his head in my lap. The soldiers run past me, chasing after Clyne.

It's good not to be the center of attention, for once.

Mr. Howe isn't even looking; a couple of parchment scrolls from the library fell from Clyne's ship. Howe quickly wraps some Thickskin around his fingers, then picks them up gingerly, almost tenderly.

I use that same kind of gentleness cradling my dad's head. I whisper to him everything will be all right.

I hope it's true.

Chapter Sixteen

Clyne: Extra Credit
— *Final Class Project: 10,271 S.E.*

4. Would you recommend this reality to other students?

The answer is as complicated as a game of Cacklaw. This is a planet where the intelligent beings aren't hatched to be raised by a community; they're born live out of their mother's body; they're born hot-blooded, and there is no predicting what they'll do.

I am fascinated by them! And terrified. Our old saying "Know an egg before you crack it" has no application here. The humans of Earth Orange are wildly unpredictable.

I hope this is taken into account when grades are assessed.

For example, I am now what they call an "outlaw" — someone who breaks the rules of a community and is therefore chased by armed enforcers. And while the mammals here claim to dislike outlaws, they make many entertainments celebrating them and retelling their stories.

I doubt they will make such an entertainment about me. Live Saurians evidently unnerve them. In fact, since the human named Howe tried to force me to stay, I've been reduced to sneaking around to fish meals of orange rinds and bird bones from the trash receptacles of private dwellings. I remain a few jumps ahead of them, but I don't know how long it will last.

Still, I will attempt to finish my homework during these short rests. If I ever return, I'll need all the credit I can get.

Especially since I will get points off for breaking nearly every school rule about time travel. Worst of all, I gave a non-Saurian use of my vessel and sent her home in my stead.

But in this case, I knew a little about the egg before I cracked it: There's a reason I sent Thea, the librarian from Alexandria, to live with you on Saurius Prime. She wasn't safe here on her own world, not in her own time, nor in Eli the Boy's. But she is intelligent and has knowledge that is worth studying; she also has an interesting idea or two of her own about the displacement of time.

I hope she receives an opportunity to explain the scrolls I sent back with her, which were salvaged from her library: They contain amazing histories of ancient cultures on Earth Orange—many of which were gone long before Alexandria was ever built—surprisingly accurate predictions about dimensions and cosmology, maps of a place called Atlantis, which no longer appears to exist either, and a whole category of literature the Earth mammals call "love poems."

I also hope Thea is afforded the opportunity to address the whole school at an assembly; not only is she fascinating, but it will help prove to everyone that I am not insane, which will be most helpful should I ever get back.

I have to stop writing now. One of the other Earth mammals—a "dog" in the local tongue—is sounding an alarm, and some humans are sure to come out of their dwelling to investigate. Better if they don't see me, so I will move on.

I don't know how I'm going to get home yet, or whether you'll send a rescue party out for me when you realize I'm not going to make it back to class. If you try to land here, it may not be pleasant.

Still, there are plenty of good beings. I will try to figure out a safe way to make contact with Eli the Boy and his father.

Until then, I will travel this surprising planet

in secret, gathering what information I can, attempting to put it all in this report. And hoping this report will someday reach you.

I am reminded of another saying I haven't thought of in years, taught to me by one of my clutch-parents when I was still a nestling: "Keep both eyes open at all times — a million worlds surround you."

Chapter Seventeen

Thea: Letters Home
Time Undetermined

Ever since Tiberius came after us, setting everything in motion in Alexandria, so much of what has happened feels like a dream. And not always a good one. But there seems to be no indication that I will wake up anytime soon.

Each new event outstrips the last: How do I adequately describe my journey with Eli, the boy wizard, who pulled me through the fabric of time itself, through the Fifth Dimension—a land of dream . . . and color . . . and longing? Longing for a time and place truly my own . . . but I doubt I will know such a place ever again.

Perhaps I should write of the brief time I spent in Eli's world, where I found out that there is no time or place in which wizards are safe from attack.

Or perhaps I should start with where I am now: a world wholly strange to me, filled entirely by lizard folk. They remind me of some of our animal gods in Alexandria—but they are not gods, of course.

They are big and mostly polite and seem to be studying me cautiously; watching my every move, jotting things down, conferring with one another. They also provide what food they can for me, which they regard as a strange diet of exotic grains and fruits.

They are still overcoming their absolute shock at seeing me emerge from K'lion's time-ship. I think some of them might have taken offense that one such as I—a creature unlike them—could even master the controls of such a vessel.

It was not hard. K'lion taught me the basics when he showed me the ship in Alexandria. And the course for "home" had already been set.

I should say the course for *K'lion's* home. Not mine. Mine is lost now.

And perhaps that is where I should focus this journal entry: on the handful of scrolls that were saved from the library.

With my mother gone, that leaves just me. The scrolls and me. We are all that remains of the great library.

But I have Mother's thirst for knowledge. And now, if my new hosts allow it, I have use of the lizard beings' time-ship. I will become an explorer on my own, reclaim the knowledge that was lost, and add new discoveries.

I will do all this in memory of Hypatia, who taught me life is a great mystery with much to know and explain.

Perhaps they will let me go look for my two lost friends, and bring Eli the wizard here, or at least K'lion. This is, after all, where he belongs.

And after a long adventure, it is good to go home.

Chapter Eighteen

Eli: Message in a Bottle

October 30, 2019 C.E.

LIZARD MAN IN THE WOODS!

It's a headline in the *National Weekly Truth*, one of the few remaining "papers" still actually printed on paper. I see it when Dad and I are standing in line at the grocery store in Glen Ellen.

It's been a few weeks now, and we occasionally get secondhand news about Clyne that way. The online *Chronicle* had its own, more serious, article called "The Return of Bigfoot," describing footprints people had seen near here. I think they were Clyne's. I hope he manages to stay safe.

A couple weeks ago he left an orange on our doorstep, with the word *Hello* carved in the peel.

Luckily, I found it before the DARPA agents did.

There are only a couple around at any given time lately. But they follow us everywhere. One is behind us in line at the grocery store now, getting ready to tail us home.

We don't see Mr. Howe much, but he uses the agents to keep tabs on us.

His current fascination is with slow pox. The situation's getting a little scary—a couple cities are on the verge of declaring quarantines.

As it turns out, that's what Mr. Howe wanted with the scrolls from the library at Alexandria. He didn't actually care what was *on* the scroll; he wanted the scroll itself, the parchment, the goatskin.

Most of the livestock back in Thea's time were carriers of slow pox, and Mr. Howe figured if he could get a sample of animal skin — like the parchment — he could extract the slow pox DNA and make his own batch.

Dad wonders if maybe that's what's causing the outbreaks in the first place. The time stream is still out of whack. Recently another plane, this time going from Chicago to Mexico City, managed to land before it actually took off, after disappearing off the radar screen. But that was so unbelievable, it wound up in the *National Weekly Truth*, too, a few days before the "Lizard Man" story about Clyne.

With all the strange things happening, Dad has a strange idea of his own: He thinks maybe Mr. Howe got his strain of slow pox perfected after all, and it escaped from the lab and caused the outbreak.

Or rather, it escaped from the lab in the near future, but strains of the disease have come back in time to start infecting us now.

I hope that doesn't mean I helped cause it by becoming unstuck in time in the first place. By messing up the time stream with my

WOMPER charge. I wonder if Dad feels that way, too. Or Mr. Howe.

No, I'm pretty sure Mr. Howe wouldn't worry about it.

Dad and I talk about that in the truck, and he tells me again and again not to blame myself. But that's what I've been telling him about Mom's disappearance, that he couldn't have known what would happen and he can't keep making himself miserable, not if there's a chance to get her back. But he doesn't buy it at all.

We get home, and the DARPA guy pulls up right behind us.

As Dad unpacks the groceries, I go to my room and check the Comnet for messages. For the first time in months, there's one from my friend Andy:

> Sorry it's been so long. I miss having you here. Strange things have been happening since you left. Like my little sister saying she's been talking to my great-grandma a lot lately. Except, my

great-grandma's been dead for years. Weird,
huh? My parents have been taking her to doctors,
but she won't change her mind. I don't even know
what my great-grandma looks like. How have you
been? How's California?

Hey, Wall, I miss you, too, I start to write
back. But I leave the reply unfinished. What
can I say? That his sister will be all right once
we get the fabric of time patched back up?
That I'm friends with a girl who's more than a
thousand years old, and that I know a talking
dinosaur, too?

How could you even tell anybody who
wasn't there?

That's the worst part of it, really. I've
become kind of a secret myself, like a part of
DARPA. Kind of a shadow, living a different
life from everyone else.

Maybe that's what Mr. Howe meant by
"Danger Boy."

The danger is getting cut off from the world

you know, because you've seen worlds no one else can even imagine.

But Andy's isn't the only message waiting for us at home.

There's a slip of paper, stationery from some old hotel, lying on the floor in Dad's lab, next to the time sphere.

It's in Mom's handwriting.

It says *Help*.

The DARPA agent sees it, too, and he's already on the phone to Mr. Howe, who I know will come rushing over now, and this might jump-start everything again.

"Dad, I have to go outside and take a walk," I tell him.

"I understand." He thinks I'm confused and upset about the note from Mom, knowing she's back there in time and knowing she wants our help.

I *am* upset and confused, but not for the reasons he thinks.

I walk down the path to the spot where

Thea and I came through the Fifth Dimension. I stand in front of the oak where I hid my Seals cap.

There seems to be so much left to do.

Help, Mom wrote.

How? When?

I tried to go back to a "regular" life after Alexandria, but maybe this is my regular life now, moving around in time.

Maybe I am Danger Boy.

I need to ask Dad a couple things first, then I'll be back for the cap.

And I'll be gone before Mr. Howe gets here.

ACKNOWLEDGMENTS

This is both my first book—and it isn't. Rather, the first "Danger Boy" adventure is finding its way back into print—and your hands—through the good offices of Candlewick Press. They are, all of them, a swell bunch, and have provided a welcome home. Under the tutelage of editor Cynthia Platt, the original story has become even more fully realized. Thank you.

And, too, the friends and family who accompany you on that journey to getting published—whether the first time or the fifteenth—all deserve a kiss and hug for their patience, good humor, and support. In particular, thanks are due to Kevin J. Foxe, Brian Lipson, and my agent, Ruth Cohen, who helped steer this book to its first contract, when it was still a combination of book proposal, early chapters, and mind's-eye glimmer. Likewise, a doff of the hat to my grandmother Lil, who loaned me some money way back in one of those starving artist phases, which allowed me to quit temping and finish my first book.

That's not the story you hold now, but its writing made this one possible. I hope, Grandma, this helps repay some of the debt.

Eli's adventures continue in Episode 2!

DANGER BOY
Dragon Sword

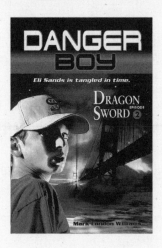

The old king stands by the lake, looking over it as for the last time, waiting.

Waiting for a woman. A woman who's never touched land.

After a moment, she appears from under the water, calmly floating up, then hovering just over the surface. The woman remains utterly serene, as if rising from a lake then standing above it were scarcely remarkable. She seems very patient, as though she could wait a long time to take tired kings into her liquid embrace, take them into the lake with her when their hearts are broken for the last time.

This king is very tired. He's seen too much war, too much bloodshed — and knows he's caused a lot of it.

When he was younger, he never thought he'd wind up hurting like this. He thought everything would be perfect.

The king is going to throw the sword into the lake, let this water sprite have it, because this sword, it seems to him now, is the root cause of all his misery.

He remembers pulling it from the rock when he was younger; he remembers thinking it would make him invincible.

That was a lie. It only made him king.

Now, no more lies. Just water. And silence.

He holds the sword above his head, ready to fling it into what he thinks will be its final resting place.

"Arthur."

It's Merlin's voice. The old wizard is always speaking at moments like this, breaking the king's concentration, never quite taking anything seriously enough.

This time Merlin's pointing. Out at the water. The serenity is even draining from the Lady of the Lake's face. There's a swirl of foam and bubbles next to her, and something unexpected. An intruder.

It was just supposed to be the king and Merlin here, alone with the water sprite, to dispose of the sword. The sword and a whole lot of bad memories.

But there's someone else. Someone who's kind of . . . fading in. Thrashing about in the water, gasping for air, trying to swim.

Is it another wizard, here to challenge Merlin? Or perhaps a spirit, the wandering ghost of some man killed by the king in a forgotten war?

The king can't tell. But Merlin doesn't seem worried. He seems, in fact, slightly amused.

But then, Merlin always seems amused, no matter how bad the situation.

The small caps and breakers in the lake are

shredded apart by the frantic splashing as the intruder buzzes through the water like a small, agitated shark.

As the trespasser draws near, the king lowers his sword and lets it rest in the mud by his leggings.

It's a boy coming to them. Out of the water. A boy.

Soon to be a man, but not quite.

About twelve years old.

Wearing jeans and a baseball cap — though the king wouldn't have the faintest idea what to call them.

"Hello," the boy finally gasps.

"Well met," the king says. "Or, perhaps, not so well. Merlin, is this one of yours?"

The boy looks from one man to the other, then back at the king. "Arthur?" The boy speaks with the strangest accent the king has ever heard.

But the conversation is interrupted. The water starts bubbling and churning again. And another boy begins fading into view.

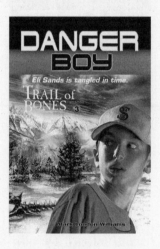

Coming next!

DANGER BOY
City of Ruins

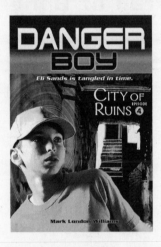

When Thea is infected by slow pox, Eli and his friends head to ancient Jerusalem to find a cure!

Mark London Williams lives in Los Angeles, where he writes articles, comics, plays, and Danger Boy books, and continues to draw inspiration from his two young sons and one old dog. In fact, when his oldest son was a toddler — long before he played his first video game — he ran down the hall one afternoon, shouting "I'm a Danger Boy!" Then he quickly added something about dinosaurs. Mark London Williams has been thanking him for *that* inspiration ever since.